THE COWBOY SEAL

BY
LAURA MARIE ALTOM

MILLS &
BOON

Published in Great Britain 2014
by Mills & Boon, an imprint of Harlequin (UK) Limited,
Eton House, 18-24 Paradise Road, Richmond, Surrey, TW9 1SR

© 2014 Laura Marie Altom

ISBN: 978-0-263-91328-6

23-1014

Harlequin (UK) Limited's policy is to use papers that are natural, renewable and recyclable products and made from wood grown in sustainable forests. The logging and manufacturing processes conform to the legal environmental regulations of the country of origin.

Printed and bound in Spain
by Blackprint CPI, Barcelona

After college (Go, Hogs!), bestselling, award-winning author **Laura Marie Altom** did a brief stint as an interior designer before becoming a stay-at-home mom to boy-girl twins and a bonus son. Always an avid romance reader, she knew it was time to try her hand at writing when she found herself replotting the afternoon soaps.

When not immersed in her next story, Laura teaches art at a local middle school. In her free time, she beats her kids at video games, tackles Mount Laundry and, of course, reads romance!

Laura loves hearing from readers at either PO Box 2074, Tulsa, OK 74101, USA, or by e-mail, balipalm@aol.com.

This story is dedicated to Dr Keith L. Stanley
and Dr Brent C. Nossaman, as well as the nurses
and staff of Tulsa Bone & Joint.
Thank you for giving me back my hand!

Chapter One

"Hey there, cowboy."

From his stool at Tipsea's crowded bar, Navy SEAL Cooper Hansen cast a sideways glance at the stacked brunette who'd slipped her arm around his shoulders.

"Buy a lady a drink?"

"Be happy to…" After tipping the brim of his raggedy straw Stetson, he nodded to the bartender. "Only I'm gonna need you to finish it over there."

When he pointed to the opposite side of the most popular squid hangout in town—her expression morphed from confusion to anger. "I should've known better than to chase after a no-good cowboy in a SEAL bar. Obviously, you don't have a clue what it's like to be a *real* man."

"Guess not." Rather than watch her go, he swigged his longneck brew, intent on enjoying his few remaining hours of freedom for what he feared could be a good, long while.

His pal and team member, Grady Matthews, took the stool alongside him. Everyone called him Sheikh due to the fact that on any given night of the week, he was surrounded by his own personal harem of beauties.

"You do know the object of hitting a bar is to go home with the pretty girl, not to run her off, right?"

After taking another deep pull, Cooper snorted. "Thanks for the advice, but given my current dark-ass mood, the only place any sane woman would want me is far away."

"There you are, Cowboy!" Another longtime friend and team member, Heath Stone, wandered up. "Everyone's looking for you. The whole point of this gathering was to give you a night so good, you don't forget to hurry back."

"I appreciate it, man—" Cooper patted his friend's shoulder "—but knowing what's ahead of me, any hellhole on the planet looks better than where I'm headed."

"Which is where? Sorry, I only paid attention to the guys'-night portion of the email." He gave him a wink and an elbow nudge. "Not that I'm complaining, but I can't remember the last time I've been out of the house. Libby keeps me on a tight leash."

"And if you don't kiss me, I'll give that leash a good, hard tug." Heath's wife, Libby, snuck up behind him to nuzzle his neck. Cooper was no expert on the whole love thing, but if he was a betting man, he'd say his friend was a goner.

While the two indulged in giggling and good, old-fashioned necking, Cooper discreetly looked away. The bar was dim and Pearl Jam loud. Tipsea's was a legend in Norfolk, and since another team member's wife purchased it, SEALs always drank free—a perk Cooper would very much miss. The grunge rock? Not so much. He was more of an old-school Hank Williams kind of guy.

His pals meant well by hosting this shindig, but the

God's honest truth was that he'd just as soon get on with things. No amount of beer or pretty women would sugarcoat the fact that what he had waiting for him back home in Brewer's Falls, Colorado, was good, old-fashioned hell.

"How's Clint doing?" Millie Hansen looked up from the stack of bills she'd been arranging in order of importance. The electric company's blaze-orange shut-off notice took precedence over the two late-payment credit card notices.

"Finally asleep." As she was near to sleepwalking herself, Millie's heart went out to her sister-in-law, Peg.

"I can't thank you enough for your help. Since Jim died…" She removed her reading glasses, blotting her eyes with her sweater sleeve—who could afford genuine tissues?

"He's my dad. Where else would I be?" She arched her head back and closed her eyes.

At 10:00 p.m. on a blustery January Monday, the old Queen Anne home shuddered from the force of the Colorado plain's wind. The desk's banker's lamp provided the office's only light. Both kids were blessedly in their rooms—Millie didn't fool herself by believing the older one was actually sleeping. Eleven-year-old LeeAnn was probably reading with the aid of a flashlight beneath her covers. J.J.—age seven—had crashed before Millie finished tucking him in.

She set her reading glasses atop her open, ledger-style checkbook. "Hate to bring up a sore subject, but did you ever hear from Cooper?"

Peg sighed. "Left a half-dozen messages. Does hearing his gruff voice mail recording count as contact?"

"What're we going to do?" During the long days spent cooking and doing the dozens of other daily chores it took to keep the ranch running, Millie didn't have time to worry, much less spare a thought for her absentee brother-in-law, Cooper. But at night, fears crept in, slithering into every vulnerable part of her soul, reminding her just how bad the past few years had been and how much worse her future could get. If they lost the ranch that'd been in the Hansen family for over a hundred years, she didn't know what they'd do—where they'd even go.

"I ask myself that question every night when I'm up pacing, because worry won't let me sleep."

"Will we make it to spring?"

Shrugging, Peg leaned forward, resting her elbows on her knees. "You know I'd stay if I could, but my savings is dwindling, and I still have a mortgage back in Denver. The hospital won't give me more leave. Come Monday, I'm expected back."

Millie swallowed the knot in her throat and nodded. "I understand."

"Dad's stable enough that I've arranged for a series of nurses and therapists to keep up with his rehabilitation here at home. His speech therapist said Dad's making all the right sounds, so with work, in between official therapy sessions, you and I should be able to help him make the right connections. Hopefully, a few neighbors will step in to help with his general care during the day."

And at night? Caring for a stroke victim was an around-the-clock job. Getting the Black Angus herd that would be their salvation come spring through what was feeling like a never-ending winter wasn't exactly your average nine-to-fiver. Then there were her kids, whom Millie already spent precious little time with. The weight of her responsibilities bore down on her shoulders, making them ache. "Lynette mentioned she'd be willing to come over anytime we need her. I'll give her a call." Lynette was Millie's best friend since kindergarten. She'd been a godsend after Jim died.

"Good. Maybe Wilma could help out some, too? I'll drive up every weekend." Wilma was a widowed neighbor who used to be in a quilting circle with the woman who would've been Millie's mother-in-law——that is, if Kay Hansen had lived long enough to see her youngest son marry. Her death was never spoken of. Her passing had launched the beginning of the Hansen family's unraveling.

EXHAUSTION FROM THE twenty-seven-hour drive did nothing to ease the acid churning in Cooper's stomach. The cold, cloudy morning cast a gray pall over his already dreary hometown.

In the twelve years since he'd been gone, nothing about Brewer's Falls had changed. Same bedraggled downtown with the century-old brick bank that also served as the post office and drugstore. Besides the feed store, Elmer's Grocery, the diner, bar and community center, no other businesses lined the only road. The few kids were bused the two-hour round trip to attend school in Wilmington.

The half-block stretch of sidewalks was weed-choked and cracked, and the few trees were bare. Hanging baskets filled with the brown ghosts of summer's bounty swung from the diner's porch.

In all of a minute's time, he'd left town to turn onto the dirt road leading to his family's ranch. He'd forgotten the plain's stark beauty, and yet he'd joined the Navy with the express purpose of finding that same beauty at sea.

The ugly-ass town with its homely jumble of buildings had no redeeming qualities other than, he supposed, the good people who lived there. A few old-timers. His little brother's widow and her kids—the nephew and niece that due to his father's hatred, Cooper had never even met.

If anything, the lonely town served as a blight upon the otherwise beautiful land. Hell, Brewer's Falls didn't even have a waterfall. The town's founder—Hawthorne Brewer—thought the idyllic name might draw in folks wanting a quieter way of life.

The road was in even worse shape than he remembered, which served his purpose well, considering the rock-strewn surface forced him to slow his pace.

The school bus passed.

Were his niece and nephew on board?

For a moment, the passing vehicle's dust cloud impeded his view, but when the dust settled, the life he'd spent years trying to forget came roaring into view.

At first, the two-story home, outbuildings and the cottonwoods his grandparents had planted were a distant speck. As they grew, so did his dread.

You're not my son, but a murderer....

Bile rose in his throat while his palms sweat and his pulse uncomfortably raced.

The Black Angus cattle that, for as long as Cooper could remember had been the ranch's lifeblood, huddled near the south pasture feeding station. The livestock's breath fogged in the cold morning air. How many mornings just like this had he ridden out at dawn to check on them?

It seemed inconceivable that he'd once felt more at ease on the back of his horse than he now did at a depth of a hundred feet.

The closer the house loomed, the more evident it became that the ranch and its occupants had fallen on hard times. His big sister, Peg—an ICU nurse who'd long since moved to Denver—was the only family he talked to. She'd told him that after his brother's death, his father had for all practical purposes shut down. Cooper had offered to return then, but Peg reported having broached the topic with their dad only to find him not just unreceptive, but downright hostile.

And so Cooper had continued his exile.

He pulled onto the house's dirt drive, holding his breath when passing the spot where basically, his life had ended. Sure, he'd worked hard and made a new family with his SEAL team, but it was his old one he mourned.

The one he'd literally and figuratively killed.

He put his truck in park, letting it idle for a minute before cutting the engine. He braced his forearms against the wheel, resting his chin atop them, staring at the house that in his mind's eye had once been the most wondrous place on earth. Now the front porch gutter sagged and over a decade's worth of summer sun had faded his mother's favorite shade of yellow paint to dirty white. Weeds choked her flower garden, and the branch holding his childhood tire swing had broken.

A dozen memories knotted his throat—cruel reminders that this was no longer his home. Per his sister's repeated requests, he'd help until his dad got back on his feet, but after that, Cooper would retreat to the haven the Navy had become.

Forcing a deep breath, he knew he could no longer put off the inevitable. From the sounds of it, his dad was in such bad shape, he wouldn't even realize his son had stepped foot in the house. By the time he did, Cooper would've worked up his courage enough to face him.

Out of his ride, he grabbed his ditty bag from the truck bed, slinging it over his shoulder.

Feet leaden, heart heavier still, he crossed the mostly dirt yard to mount steps he'd last tread upon when he'd essentially been a boy. The Navy had honed him into a man, but confronting his past eroded his training like ocean waves ripping apart a fragile shore.

It all came rushing back.

That god-awful night when he'd done the unthinkable. His sister's screams. His brother's and father's stoic stares. The funeral. The guilt that clung tight to this day.

"Cooper?"

He looked up to find his sister-in-law, his little brother's high school sweetheart, clutching her tattered blue robe closed at the throat.

He removed his hat, pinning it to his chest. "Hey…"

"What're you doing here? I thought— I'm sorry. Where are my manners?" She held open the front door. "Get in here before you catch your death of cold."

He brushed past her, hyperaware of the light floral fragrance she'd worn since her sixteenth birthday when his brother had gifted it to her, declaring her to be the prettiest girl he knew. Millie was no longer pretty, but beautiful. Her hair a deep chestnut, and her haunted gaze as blue as a spring sky, despite dark circles shadowing her eyes. He couldn't help but stare. Catching himself, hating that his face grew warm, he sharply looked away.

The contrast of the front room's warmth to the outside chill caused him to shiver. He'd forgotten a real winter's bite.

"I—I can't believe you're here." She'd backed onto the sofa arm—the same sofa he used to catch her and Jim making out on. She fussed with her hair, looking at him, then away. "Peg tried calling so many times…."

"Sorry." He set his ditty bag on the wood floor, then shrugged out of his Navy-issued pea jacket to hang it on the rack near the door. He'd have felt a damn sight better with his hat back on, but his mother had never allowed hats in the house, so he hung it alongside his coat. "I've been out of town." Syria had been *lovely* this time of year. "Guess I should've called, but…"

"It's okay. I understand."

Did she? Did she have a clue what it had been like for him to one day belong to a loving, complete family and the next to have accidentally committed an act so heinous, his own father never spoke to him again?

"You're here now, and that's what matters."

"Yeah…" Unsure what to do with his hands, he crammed them into his pockets.

"I imagine you want to see your dad?"

He sharply exhaled. "No. Hell, no."

"Then why did you come?"

"Peg said you need me."

She chewed on that for a moment, then shook her head. "I needed you when Jim died, too. Where were you then?"

"Aw, come on, Mill… You know this is complicated."

Skimming his hands over his buzz-cut hair, he turned away from her and sighed. "Got any coffee?"

"Sure."

He followed her into the kitchen, momentarily distracted by the womanly sway of her hips. Two kids had changed her body, but for the better. He liked her with a little meat on her bones—not that it was his place to assess such a thing. She'd always been—would always be—his brother's girl.

She handed him a steaming mug.

He took a sip, only to blanch. "You always did make awful coffee. Good to see that hasn't changed."

Her faint smile didn't reach blue eyes glistening with unshed tears. "I can't believe you're really here."

"In the flesh."

"How long are you staying?"

"Long as you need me." Or at least until his dad regained his faculties enough to kick him out again. To this day, his father's hatred still burned, but the worst part of all was that Cooper didn't blame him. Hell, the whole reason he worked himself so damned hard during the day was so exhaustion granted some small measure of peace at night.

"You haven't changed a bit," she noted from behind her own mug. "I always could see the gears working in your mind."

"Yeah?" He dumped his coffee down the drain then started making a fresh pot. "Tell me, swami, what am I thinking?"

"About her." She crept up behind him, killing him when she slipped her arms around his waist for a desperately needed, but undeserved hug. Her kindness made it impossible to breathe, to think, to understand that after all this time, why he was even here. "It's okay, Coop." She rested her forehead between his shoulder blades. Her warm exhalations sent shock waves through his T-shirt then radiating across his back. "I mean, obviously it's not okay, but you have to let it go. Your mom was so kind. She'd hate seeing you this way."

A dozen years' grief and anger and heartache balled inside him, threatening to shatter. Why was Millie being nice? Why didn't she yell or condemn him for staying away? Why didn't she do anything other than give him the comfort he'd so desperately craved?

"Coop, look at me...." Her small hands tugged him around to face her, and when she used those hands to cup his cheeks while her gaze locked with his, he couldn't for a second longer hold in his pain. What was he doing here? No matter what Peg said, he never should've come. "Honey, yes, what happened was awful, but it was an accident. Everyone knows that. No one blames you."

A sarcastic laugh escaped him. "Have you met my father?"

"When your mom died, he was out of his mind with grief. He didn't know what he was saying or doing. I'll bet if you two talked now, then—"

"How are we going to do that? The man suffered a stroke."

"That doesn't mean he can't listen. At least give it a try. You owe yourself that much."

How could she say that after what he'd done? The world—let alone his father—didn't owe him shit. "Coming here—it was a mistake. I never should've—"

"You're wrong, Cooper. Your dad may not admit it, but he needs you. I need you." She stepped back to gesture to the dilapidated kitchen with its outdated appliances, faded wallpaper and torn linoleum floor. "This place needs you."

He slammed the filter drawer shut on the ancient Mr. Coffee. "More than you could ever know, I appreciate your kind words, Mill, but seriously? What does anyone need with a guy who killed his own mother?"

Chapter Two

Millie's mind still reeled from the fact that her husband's brother was even in the room, let alone the fact that he was here to stay awhile. His mere presence was a godsend. While she considered the tragedy that'd caused his mother's death to be ancient history, for him it seemed time had stood still. Had he even begun to process the fact Jim was gone, too?

Before the coffee finished brewing, he pulled out the glass pot, replacing it with his mug. With it only half-full, he replaced the pot.

"Better?" she found the wherewithal to ask after he'd downed a good portion of the brew.

"Much." His faint smile reminded her so much of her lost love that her heart skipped a beat. It'd been three years since she'd lost Jim, and while she thought of him often—would never forget him—in the time he'd been gone, more urgent matters occupied the space grief had once filled in her heart.

"Hungry?" she asked. "The kids got oatmeal, but if you want, I'll cook you up something more substantial." Busying her flighty hands, she rummaged through the fridge. "There's a little bacon. We always have plenty of eggs. Pancakes? Do you still like them?"

"Coffee's fine," he said with a wag of his mug. He looked her up and down, then politely aimed his stare out the kitchen window. "Judging by your outfit, you haven't done any of the outside chores?"

She reddened, clutching the robe close at her throat.

"I assume the routine hasn't changed?"

"No, but you're probably tired from your drive. Why don't you nap for a bit, and after I check on your dad, I'll head outside."

"No need. Fresh air will do me good."

"You do know you're eventually going to have to see him."

"Dad?"

"The Easter Bunny…"

He finished his coffee then put the mug in the sink. "Not if I can help it." He nodded to the tan Carhartt hanging on a hook by the back door. "Mind if I borrow that?"

"Help yourself." The duster-style coat had belonged to Jim. Sometimes when she felt particularly overwhelmed, she wore it to remind her of him. It used to smell of him—the trace of the tobacco he'd chewed. How many times had she scolded him to quit, afraid of losing him to cancer when instead he'd passed from a hunting accident?

"Was this my brother's?"

Swallowing the knot in her throat, she nodded.

She wanted to rail on him for not having had the common decency—the respect—to attend Jim's funeral, but she lacked the strength to argue.

"About that…"

"J-just go, Cooper." She didn't want to hear what he had to say, because no mere explanation would ever be good enough. No matter what, a man didn't miss his own brother's funeral. Just didn't happen.

The set of his stubbled square jaw was grim, but then so was the inside of her battered heart. Peg might've told him what the past few years without her husband had been like for Millie, but he didn't really know. Beyond the financial toll Jim's death had taken, emotionally, she felt as if a spring twister had uprooted every aspect of her and her kids' lives. And speaking of her kids, they'd never even had the pleasure of meeting their uncle Cooper.

"Okay..." he mumbled.

Never-ending seconds stretched between them. Her watering eyes refused to quit stinging, and her frayed nerves itched for a fight.

"Thanks for the coffee. Guess I'll head outside."

Only after he'd gone, leaving her with just the wall of brutal January air to prove he'd ever even been in the room, did Millie dare exhale.

From a workload standpoint, having Cooper back on the ranch might be a godsend, but would it be worth the emotional toll?

"HEY, GIRL..." COOPER approached Sassy, the sorrel mare he'd been given for his eighteenth birthday. At the time, working this ranch, finding a good woman, having kids, had been all he'd ever wanted from life. Strange how even though he'd accomplished and seen more than he ever could've dreamed, he still felt like that kid who'd been run off in shame. "Long time, no see, huh?"

He stroked her nose and was rewarded by a warm, breathy snort against his palm. For this weather, he

should've worn gloves and a hat, but pride won over
common sense when he'd scurried for the barn's safety.

Regardless of where things stood with his father,
Cooper knew damn well he'd done wrong by his brother
and sweet Millie.

It'd been ages since he'd saddled a horse, and it took
a while to get his bearings. Having followed the routine since he'd been a kid, he knew the drill, just had to
reacquaint himself with where everything was stored.
He found leather work gloves that'd seen better days
and a hat that looked like a horse had stomped it to
death before it'd wrestled with a tractor. Regardless,
he slapped it on his head, thankful for the warmth, but
wishing the simple work didn't leave his mind with so
much space to wander.

Millie wasn't flashy.

Hell, back in Virginia Beach, she wasn't the sort
of woman to whom he'd have given a second glance.
Funny thing was, back at Tipsea's, he'd only been on
the prowl for one thing, and it sure wouldn't have made
his momma proud. A woman like Millie, who was as
at home in a big country kitchen as she was out on the
range, was the kind of catch a man could be proud to
escort to a Grange Hall dance.

His brother had been damned lucky to have found
someone like Millie so young. Little good it'd done him,
though, seeing how he'd gone and died way before his
time. What'd Jim been thinking, shooting from a mov-
ing four-wheeler? Had disaster written all over it.

*Yeah? How many shots you taken from a Mark V at
fifty knots, yet you're still ticking?*

Jim may have been hot-dogging, but it wasn't a
stunt Cooper hadn't tried himself. Only difference

was that Cooper had gone fast enough for the devil not to catch up.

Even when they'd been kids, Millie had been a feisty little thing. He couldn't even imagine the fury she'd had with her husband for putting himself in that position. With two kids, he should've known better.

But then who was Cooper to talk?

His entire adult life had been based on a split-second nightmare from which he still hadn't awoken.

"How are you this morning?" Millie asked her father-in-law, even though she knew he couldn't respond.

He replied with a snarling growl.

To say Clint was having a tough time adjusting to his new reality was putting it mildly. Poor guy had been a powerhouse all his life. He was making progress in his recovery, but it was far too slow for his liking.

Millie hustled through the personal-hygiene routine Peg taught her to follow. The nurse would handle his primary bathing, but no matter how much her father-in-law clearly resented Millie invading his personal space, for his own well-being, the job needed to be done.

"You should've seen your naughty granddaughter trying to get out of school this morning." While brushing Clint's teeth, she kept up a line of running chatter. She couldn't tell if her attempt at levity had any effect on the patient, but it at least helped calm her nerves. "It's cold enough out there, we might have to break the smoke off the chimney."

All her good cheer earned was another grunt.

"Your new therapist should be here after a while. I think she'll be working on speech today. Peg's got a whole slew of folks coming out to help." She tidied his bedding. "It's gonna be a regular Grand Central Station 'round here."

More grumbling erupted from Clint, but she ignored him in favor of slipping his small whiteboard around his neck, along with the attached dry-erase marker. It was a struggle for him to smoothly move his right arm and hand, but as with the rest of his recovery, with each passing day he grew more adept at the skill.

"Now that you're all cleaned up, I'm going to make your breakfast then be right back."

She prepared a light meal of scrambled eggs with cheese and pureed peaches. Clint loved coffee, so she filled a lidded mug with the steaming liquid then added a few ice cubes before sealing the top and adding a straw. Would he notice it wasn't her usual awful brew?

Peg said Clint's hearing was fine.

Had he heard Cooper enter the house?

Millie didn't have long to wait for an answer. She entered Clint's room only to find he'd already been practicing his writing. On his board were the barely legible letters: *C-O-O-P?*

His bloodshot eyes begged for an answer that left her wishing they'd found a way to install Clint's hospital-style bed in the upstairs master bedroom as opposed to Kay's old sewing room.

How much had Clint heard?

With an extra cantankerous growl, he waved the board hard enough to send the attached marker flying on its string. The writing instrument landed smack dab in the center of Clint's eggs, which only made him roar louder.

Jerking the marker back as if it were on a yo-yo

string, he drew a line through his former word to painstakingly write: *O-U-T!*

"WHO ARE YOU?"

After a long day of checking the well-being of not just the cattle, but fencing and the overall state of the land, as well, Cooper had just finished brushing his horse when a pretty, freckle-faced girl, whose braids reminded him an awful lot of Millie's back when she'd been a kid, raised her chin and scowled.

"Mom doesn't like strangers messing with our livestock."

The fire flashing behind her sky-blue eyes also reminded him of her momma. "You must be LeeAnn?"

"Yeah?" Eyes narrowed, she asked, "Who are you, and how do you know my name?"

A boy peeked out from behind the partially closed door. He had the same red hair Jim had had when he'd been about that age. Jim Junior? Or J.J., as Peg more often called him. Through emails, Cooper had seen the kids' pictures, but they hadn't done them justice.

His throat grew uncomfortably tight.

How proud his brother must've been of these two, which only made his actions all the more undecipherable. If Cooper possessed such treasure, he'd be so careful….

But then he'd treasured his mother and look what'd happened to her.

Cooper pulled himself together, removed his right glove, then cautiously approached his niece, holding out his hand for her to shake. "LeeAnn, J.J., sorry it's taken me so long to finally meet you. I'm your uncle Cooper."

"The Navy SEAL?" Seven-year-old J.J. found his

courage and bolted out from his hiding spot. "Dad said you blow up ships and scuba dive and other cool stuff."

Judging by LeeAnn's prepubescent scowl, she wasn't impressed. "Mom said you abandoned your family when we needed you most."

How did he respond? Millie had only spoken the truth.

From behind him, Sassy snorted.

"You didn't ride her, did you?" His pint-size nemesis followed him on his trek to the feed bin. "Because if you did, don't *ever* do it again. Sassy's *mine*."

"Interesting…" He scooped grain into a bucket. The faint earthy-sweet smell brought him back to a time when he'd been LeeAnn and J.J.'s age. Everything had been so simple then. Do his chores, his homework, play with the dog. Speaking of which, he hadn't seen their mutt, Marvel. Not a good sign. "Because Sassy was a birthday present for me."

"You've gotta be like a hundred," his nephew noted.

Most days, I feel like it. "Only seventy-five."

"That's still pretty old…."

His niece narrowed her eyes. "That's not true. I heard Mom talking to Aunt Peg about Grandpa, and she said he was in his seventies. That means you can't be that old—probably just like fifty."

Cooper laughed. "Yeah, that's closer."

LeeAnn wrenched the feed bucket from him. "Since she's my horse, I'll take care of her."

"Be my guest." Cooper backed away. "But since I'll be here awhile, do you think we might work out a deal?"

"Like what?" She stroked the horse's nose.

"Sassy's allowed to help me with the cattle while

you're at school, then she's all yours once you get home?"

"Sounds good to me." J.J. took an apple from his backpack and sat on a hay bale to eat it, all the while watching the negotiation with rapt interest.

The girl nibbled her lower lip. Another trait she'd inherited from her mom. "I'll think about it."

"Fair enough."

"LeeAnn! J.J.!" Millie called from the house.

"Bye!" Jim's son bolted.

His sister chased after him.

Cooper gave Sassy one last pat, made sure the three other horses had plenty of food and water, then closed up the barn for the night. As the day had wound on, the weather had only grown more ugly. At five, clouds were so heavy that it was almost dark. Sleet pelted his nose and cheeks on his walk across the yard.

As miserably cold as the day had been and night now was, Cooper would've preferred to spend the evening in his truck rather than go back into the house. He didn't belong there. At least in Virginia, he'd been part of a well-oiled team.

On the ranch, he wasn't sure what he was. No-good son. Disrespectful brother. Forgotten uncle.

"Coop?"

He glanced out from beneath his hat brim to find Millie hollering at him from the back porch. Much like she had with her robe, she now clutched the lapels of a chunky brown sweater. Wind whipped her long hair, and when she drew it back, she looked so lovely in the golden light spilling from the house that his breath caught in his throat.

Lord, what was wrong with him? Appraising his

brother's wife? There was a special place in hell for men like him.

"Hurry, before your feet freeze to the yard!"

He did hurry, but only because he didn't want her hanging around outside waiting for him.

"Thanks." He brushed past her, hating that he once again noticed her sweet floral smell. He removed his hat and stood there for a sec, adjusting to not only the kitchen's warmth, but also the sight of the space filled with industrious bodies.

J.J. sat at the round oak table, frowning at an open math book. LeeAnn sat alongside him, making an unholy mess with an ugly papier-mâché mountain.

Millie had left him and now stood at the sink, washing broccoli. "Pardon the clutter. LeeAnn's volcano is due soon, and J.J. has a math test tomorrow. I heard you all formally met in the barn?"

"Yes, ma'am." What else should he say? That she'd raised a couple of fine-looking kids? That he was an ass and coward for not meeting them before now? Instead, he glanced back to the table and said the first stupid thing that popped into his head. "That's supposed to be a volcano?"

The second he asked the question, he regretted it. His few hastily spoken words ruined the bucolic family scene.

His pretty niece leaped up from the table, then dashed from the room.

"It's an *awesome* volcano!" J.J. declared before throwing his pencil at Cooper, then also leaving the room.

"I realize you've probably never been around kids," Millie said, "but you might try digging around in your big, tough Army Guy head to look for a sensitivity gene. LeeAnn's worked really hard on her science project. You didn't have to tear her down." Having delivered his tongue-lashing, Millie chased after her brood.

From upstairs came the sound of a door slamming, then muffled tears.

Son of a biscuit...

He slapped his hat onto the back-door rack and shrugged out of his brother's coat, hanging it up, too. Then he just stood there, woefully unsure what to do with his frozen hands or confused heart.

"For the record," he said under his breath, "I'm a Navy Guy."

Chapter Three

Millie held her arms around her sobbing daughter, rocking her side to side from where they sat on the edge of the bed. "Honey, he didn't mean it. You're going to have the best volcano your school's ever seen."

"I'll help, Lee." Sweet-tempered J.J. cozied up to his sister's other side. Since their father died, both kids had grown infinitely more sensitive. Millie knew one of these days she'd need to toughen them to the ways of the world, but not quite yet. They'd already been through enough. She couldn't even comprehend what would happen if they also lost their grandpa or the only home they'd ever known.

A knock sounded on the door frame.

She glanced in that direction to find Cooper taking up far too much room. He was not only tall, but his shoulders were broad, too. Back when they'd been teens, he'd been a cocky, self-assured hothead who'd never lacked for the company of a blonde, brunette or redhead. When he'd spent weekends calf-roping, rodeo buckle bunnies swarmed him like hummingbirds to nectar. She'd far preferred her even-tempered Jim. Cooper had always been just a little too *wild*.

"Make him go away," LeeAnn mumbled into Millie's shoulder.

"Look…" Cooper rammed his hands into his jeans pockets. "I'm awfully sorry about hurting your feelings."

"No, you're not!"

"LeeAnn…" Millie scolded. While she certainly didn't agree with her brother-in-law's ham-handed actions, she didn't for a moment believe him deliberately cruel. He spent all his time around mercenary types. She honestly wasn't even sure what a Navy SEAL did. Regardless, she was reasonably certain he hadn't spent a lot of time around kids.

"I really am sorry." The farther he ventured into the ultragirly room with its pink-floral walls, brass bed piled with stuffed animals and antique dressing table and bench Millie had picked up for a song at a barn auction, the more out of his element Cooper looked. "Ever heard of Pompeii?"

"I saw a movie on it," J.J. said.

"Cool." Cooper's warm, sad, unsure smile touched Millie's heart. He was trying to be a good uncle, but that was kind of hard when jumping in this late in the game. He took his phone from his back pocket then a few seconds later, handed it to her son. "This pic is of me and a few friends. We had some downtime and toured through the ruins."

"Whoa…" J.J.'s eyes widened. "That's awesome! You really were there."

"Doesn't make him like some kind of volcano expert," LeeAnn noted.

"I've always wanted to see Pompeii…" Millie couldn't help but stare in wonder at the photo. Beyond the three smiling men stretched a weathered street frozen in time. Snow-capped Mount Vesuvius towered in the background. The scene was all at once chilling, yet intriguing. The place seemed inconceivably far from Brewer's Falls.

"It was amazing but also sad." He flipped through more pics, some taken of the former citizens who had turned to stone. "Anyway... LeeAnn, you're right, I'm not even close to being a volcano expert, but if you wouldn't mind, I'd love lending a hand with your project. I wire a mean explosive and between the two of us, we could probably muster some impressive concussive force."

While both kids stared, Millie pressed her lips tight. *Concussive force?* He did realize the science fair was being held in an elementary school gym and not Afghanistan? Still, she appreciated his willingness to at least try helping her daughter. Lord knew, her own volcano-building skills were lacking. "That sounds nice," she said to her brother-in-law, "only you might scale down the eruption."

"Gotcha." He half smiled. "Small eruptions."

For only an instant, their gazes locked, but that was long enough to leave her knowing he still unnerved her in a womanly way. It'd been three long years since she'd lost her husband, and as much as she'd told herself— and her matchmaking friend, Lynette—she had no interest in dating, something about Cooper had always exuded raw sex appeal. It wasn't anything deliberate on his part, it just *was*. Had always been. Because she'd been happy with Jim, she'd studied Cooper's escapades from afar. But here, now, something about the way his lips stroked the perfectly innocuous word, *eruptions,* sent her lonely, yearning body straight to the gutter.

Her mind, on the other hand, stayed strong. If she ever decided to start dating, she'd steer far clear of anyone remotely like her brother-in-law!

"J.J., hon," the boy's mother asked an hour later from across the kitchen table, "will you say grace?"

"Yes, ma'am." He bowed his head. "God is great, God is good…"

While the boy finished, Cooper discreetly put down his fork, pretending he hadn't already nabbed a bite. The last time he'd prayed before a meal had been the last night he'd been in this house.

He looked up just as J.J. muttered *Amen,* to find Millie staring. Damn, she'd grown into a fine-looking woman. And damn, how he hated even noticing the fact.

Conversation flowed into a river of avoidance, meandering past dangerous topics such as his brother or father. Meatloaf passing and the weather took on inordinate levels of importance.

This suited Cooper just fine. He had no interest in rehashing the past and lacked the courage to wander too far into the future. His only plan was to keep things casual then head back to Virginia ASAP to rejoin his SEAL team.

"Uncle Cooper?" J.J. asked. The kid sported a seriously cute milk mustache.

"Yeah?"

"How come you didn't visit Grandpa with us tonight while he ate his dinner?"

Whoosh. Just like that, his lazy river turned into a raging waterfall, culminating in a pool of boiling indigestion. He messed with his broccoli. "I, ah, needed to clean up before your mom's tasty dinner."

"Okay." Apparently satisfied with Cooper's answer, the child reached across the table for a third roll.

His niece wasn't about to take his answer at face value. "I heard Aunt Peg and Mom talking about how much you *hate* Grandpa and he *hates* you."

"LeeAnn!" Millie set her iced tea glass on the table hard enough to rattle the serving platters. "Apologize to your uncle."

"Wh-why do you hate Grandpa?" J.J. asked, voice cracking as he looked from his uncle to his mom. "I love him a whole lot."

Son of a biscuit...

"Millie..." Cooper set his fork by his plate and pushed back his chair. "Thanks for this fine meal, but I've got to run into town. Please leave the dishes for me, and I'll wash 'em later."

"WHAT'S HE GONNA do in town?" LeeAnn asked, carrying on with her meal as if nothing had even happened. "Everything's closed."

Cooper had already left out the front door.

Millie covered her face with her hands. At this time of night, there was only one thing a man could do in Brewer's Falls—drink.

"Mom?" J.J. pressed. "What's Uncle Cooper gonna do? And why does he hate Grandpa?"

At that moment, Millie was the one hating Cooper for running out on her yet again. But then wait—during her initial crisis after she'd first lost Jim, he hadn't even bothered to show up.

"Mom?"

"J.J., *hush!*" She never snapped at her kids, but this was one time she needed space to think, breathe. She got up from the table and delivered a hasty apology before running for the stairs.

In her room, she tossed herself across the foot of the bed she and Jim had shared. Never had she needed him more. His quiet strength and logic and calm in the face of any storm.

She wanted—needed—so badly to cry, but tears wouldn't come.

Frustration for her situation balled in her stomach, punching with pain. If she had a lick of sense, she'd do the adult thing—pull herself together and join her children downstairs. She needed to play a game with them and clean the kitchen. Do research on how to build a science-fair volcano. Play mix and match with which bills she could afford to pay. Check on Clint to see if he needed anything.

While she *needed* to do all of that, what she *wanted* was an indulgent soak in the hall bathroom's claw-foot tub.

COOPER SAUNTERED INTO the smoky bar, taking a seat on a counter stool. In all the years he'd lived in the one-horse town, he'd never been in the old place. Not much to look at with twenty or so country-type patrons, dim lighting, honky-tonk-blaring jukebox, a few ratty pool tables and neon beer signs decorating the walls. But as long as the liquor bit, that'd get the job of escaping—even for a moment—done. After a few drinks, he probably wouldn't even mind the yeast scent of a quarter-century's worth of stale beer that'd sloshed onto the red industrial-style carpet.

He said to the guy behind the bar, "Shot of Jim Beam, please."

"I'll be damned… Cooper?"

"Mr. Walker?" *Seriously?* Talk about jumping from the frying pan into the fire. The grizzled cowboy not only happened to be one of his father's best friends, but owned the land adjoining the Hansen ranch.

He extended his hand for Cooper to shake. "Please, call me Mack. Figure if you're old enough to drink and serve our country, you're old enough for us to be on a first-name basis." He poured Cooper's shot then one for himself. Raising it, he said, "About time you came home."

"Only temporarily…" Cooper downed the fiery elixir. "I'll head back to my base just as soon as things get settled."

"By *things,* I assume you're talking about your father? Damn shame. Everyone's just sick about the run of bad luck your family's been having."

In no mood to hash over the past or present, Cooper wagged his glass. "Another."

Mack obligingly poured. "Things that bad out there, huh?"

Cooper winced from the liquor's bite.

"I told your father he was a damned fool for running you off. What happened with your momma… Straight-up accident that could've happened to any one of us. I know deep in his heart Clint agrees, but he's too damned stubborn to tell anyone—let alone his first-born—any different."

The tears stinging Cooper's eyes hurt worse than the liquor burning his throat.

"He needs you. Millie needs you. Hell, even those

ragtag kids of hers need you. Yep…" He smacked the wood counter. "'Bout damned time you came home."

Nice sentiment, but for his own sanity, Cooper knew he was only passing through. A long time ago he'd lost his home, his way, and for a messed-up guy like him, there was no such thing as second chances.

"WHERE'VE YOU BEEN?" Millie warmed her hands in front of the living room's woodstove, wishing she hadn't been on edge ever since Cooper had run off, vowing she wouldn't lower herself to even turn around and look at him. She thought her lazy, twenty-minute soak would make her feel better, but all it had done was given her the privacy needed to think—not good for a woman in her condition. Hot water, plus loneliness, plus closing her eyes to envision the first handsome face she'd seen in years had proven anything but relaxing. Especially when that face belonged to her dead husband's brother!

"Where do you think?"

She knew exactly where he'd been. She shouldn't have wasted the breath needed to ask. "It was a serious dick move for you to walk out like that. You owe your niece and nephew an explanation."

"*Dick move?* Talk to your momma with that mouth?"

She spun around to face him, only to find him unnervingly close. "You know better than most anyone I don't even have a mom, so you can put that sass back in your pocket."

"Sorry." He held up his hands in surrender, and her stupid, confused heart skipped a beat. The only reason she even found him attractive was the endearing similarities he'd shared with his brother. Mossy-green eyes and the faint rise in the bridge of his nose. The way his lips looked pouty when he said his m's. The way he made her wistful and achy and irrationally mad about how perfect her life had once been and no longer was. "You're right. I shouldn't have taken off, but honestly?" He shook his head, and his crooked smile further lessened her anger's hold. "I was scared." He removed his battered straw cowboy hat, crossing the room to hang it on the rack by the door. Even with his buzz cut, he sported a wicked case of hat hair and damn if it didn't look good. "Those kids of yours asked tough questions. I don't even know the answers for myself."

"I get that, but they're kids. They weren't even born when your mom died, and they take it personally when their only uncle never even had the decency to send them a birthday card. They're smart, Coop. Their little ears pick up more than I'd like, and as much as Peg loves you, she's also that exasperated by your disappearing act."

"I didn't just—"

"Shh!" she admonished when he'd gotten too loud. "Do you want to wake J.J. and LeeAnn? Even worse— your dad?"

"Sorry," he said in a softer tone. He sat hard on the sofa, cradling his forehead in his hands. "But you know damn well I didn't just *disappear.* When you run down your mother with a truck, then your father tells you to, and I quote—*Get the hell out of my house and don't ever come back*—it tends to linger on a man's soul." When he looked up, even by the light of the room's only lamp, she could tell his eyes had welled. She hated to see him hurting, but she'd hurt, too. They all had. They all were, still. He didn't own the rights to pain.

"Look…" With every part of her being, she wanted

to go to him. Sit beside him and slip her arm around his shoulders, but she physically couldn't. Her feet literally wouldn't move. Outside, sleet pelted century-old windows. The weatherman out of Denver said they could have six inches of snow by morning. "I smoothed things over with the kids by giving them an abridged version of what happened with their grandmother. But for your own well-being, you have to once and for all get it through your thick head that the only one who blames you for the accident is your father—well, aside from yourself. Why did your mom even go out there? She knew better."

A laugh as cold as the wind rattling the shutters escaped him. "Her dying words were that she'd run outside to give me a piece of her mind for drinking and staying out so late. She then told me if she'd had a lick of sense, she'd have gone to bed early in case she needed to bail me out of the county jail come morning."

"There you go. So see? She admitted she was partially to blame. Do you honestly think that just because of your cantankerous father she'd have expected you to carry this ache inside you for all these—"

A crash of metal erupted from the back bedroom where Clint was supposed to be sleeping. Then came a gut-wrenching growl.

"What was that?" Cooper asked, already on his feet, heading in that direction.

Her stomach knotted. "I would imagine, *that* was your father...."

Chapter Four

"Go see him," Millie said. "You can't avoid Clint forever."

Cooper knew she was right. Sooner or later he'd have to make peace with his father. Or at the very least, for Millie and her kids' sake, forge some semblance of civility between them. But how did he start? It wasn't as if the walls of grief standing between them could be broken with a mere apology.

Another growl rose above the stove's crackling fire and wind rattling the shutters.

"Cooper…" His sister-in-law's condemning stare made him feel all of twelve. He'd felt more comfortable staring down a shark. Her intense stare conveyed more than a day's worth of words. It told him loud and clear that until he at least spoke with his father, she wouldn't grant him a moment's peace.

"Aw, hell…" He brushed past her, hating the cramped space forcing them together. His arm didn't stop tingling from where they'd touched till he reached the end of the hall.

Cooper forced a deep breath then knocked on the closed door of his mom's old sewing room—the only possible downstairs place where Millie and his sister could have stashed his ailing father.

Rather than wait for an answer, his pulse taking the cadence of a rapid-fire machine gun, Cooper thrust open the door. He'd literally dreaded this moment for the past twelve years. "You still got a problem with me, old man?"

Clint launched a new series of growls then pitiful, racking coughs.

"You've got to calm down," Millie said, already tidying the mess her patient had made by toppling his rolling metal tray. "I meant to tell you earlier that Cooper had come for a visit, but it must've slipped my mind."

The cantankerous old man thrashed as best he could then settled when Millie took a plastic water cup from the nightstand and held the straw to his dried and cracked lips.

Cooper had readied himself for a fight with the man he used to know. The barrel-chested, ham-fisted, mean-as-a-cornered-rattler father who'd sent him packing. What he faced was a pathetic shadow of Cooper's memories. Make no mistake, judging by his scowl and dark glare, Clint still wasn't a teddy bear. But he had lost a good fifty pounds, and his complexion was as pale as the threadbare sheets and quilts covering his bed.

Clint's current condition left Cooper's eyes stinging.

He'd steeled himself for battle with a lion, not a lamb.

"There you go," Millie soothed. "It's medicine time, and I'll bet you thought I forgot you." After kissing the old man's forehead, she fished three tablets from three different prescription bottles, patiently helping Clint one at a time down them all with more water. When he signaled that he had drunk his fill, she covered his lips with ointment. "Feel better?"

The old man had his dry-erase board slung around his neck. With his good hand he wrote *O-U-T* then underlined it twice before pointing in Cooper's general direction.

Instantaneously, Cooper's anger was replaced by profound sadness. And a jolt of something he never in a million years would've expected—a fierce longing to make things right with this man he'd once so deeply loved. His mind's eye no longer replayed their last night together, but flashes of Clint patiently teaching him to change his truck's oil or beaming with pride when Cooper won his first rodeo. Then came a myriad of shared holidays and ordinary Tuesday-night suppers and racing his brother, Jim, off the school bus, both of them running as fast as they could to find out what their father had been up to in the barn. His dad had taught Cooper how to shoot a rifle, smoke cigars and treat women. What Clint hadn't done was prepare his son for how to let him go.

Which meant that in addition to saving this ragtag old ranch, Cooper now felt responsible for saving his dad.

He felt obligated to say as much, but instead, clung to the room's shadows. Gratitude for Millie knotted his throat while she fussed with his father's pillows and blankets. Cooper should've helped her. After all, the patient was his dad. But his boots felt nailed to the wood floor.

Millie asked, "What did you do with the remote to your TV?"

Cooper had only just noticed the ancient model set

atop the dresser. The volume had been turned all the way down on The Weather Channel's forecaster. Another pleasant memory accosted him when he thought back to the time he and Jim had helped Clint with their first satellite dish. Exciting didn't begin to cover how awesome it'd been to have hundreds of channels—not that their mom ever let them and Peg watch as much TV as they'd have liked.

"What're you smiling about?" Millie asked, on her knees, using a towel to sop water from his father's spilled plastic pitcher.

Cooper knelt to help, taking the towel from her. "Remember when we got MTV?"

She sat back on her haunches and frowned. "How could I forget? That was around the same time you asked why my boobs were smaller than everyone else's."

Cooper winced. "Wasn't it enough retribution for you that because of that comment, Mom made me scrub baseboards for a week?"

"No."

By the time they finished cleaning, Clint had drifted off to sleep and softly snored.

"Looks like his meds finally kicked in." Millie fished the TV remote from where it had fallen under the bed.

"Yeah…" Cooper stood there like a dope, holding the damp towel they'd used for the floor, watching Millie as she finished cleaning the last of his old man's mess.

The past bore down on Cooper's shoulders, making every inch of him ache—not just his body, but soul. He'd lost so much. His mom. Jim. And now, for all practical purposes, his dad.

That sting was back behind his eyes.

Cooper couldn't remember the last time he'd broken down—maybe not since that long ago awful night. "I—I've gotta get out of here."

Planning an escape to the barn, he pitched the towel on the kitchen table before making a beeline for the back door. But before he could get it open, Millie was there, wrapping her arms around him, holding strong through his emotional fall.

His tears were ugly and all-consuming, making his muscles seize. Though he had no right, Cooper clung to Millie, breathing her in. She smelled good and familiar. Of everything he'd left and tried so hard to forget, but clearly had not yet succeeded.

"I—I'm sorry," he managed after finally getting ahold of himself. "Shit…" He released her to rake his fingers through his hair. "I'm not even sure what just happened."

"Something that probably needed to happen back when your mom died? And again, for your brother?" She rubbed her hand along his upper arm. "Plus, it can't have been easy—finding your dad in that condition."

"Stop making excuses." Not wanting her to see him, he turned to the wall, planting his palms flat against the cool plaster, then his forehead.

She stepped behind him. He knew, because he sensed her. Felt her heat. When she kneaded his shoulders, he closed his eyes and groaned. "Lord, that feels good."

"I'm glad."

"You should stop."

"Why?" She worked her thumbs between his shoulder blades.

"Because I don't deserve your comfort any more than you've deserved to be stuck here on your own with this mess."

"This *mess* you refer to happens to be your father. The man who taught me to cook a mean elk steak and nursed me through losing my husband." She stopped giving Cooper pleasure to instead urge him around. Her pained expression, the unshed tears shining in her eyes, made the whiskey lingering in his gut catch fire.

He winced from the sudden pang.

Something in her expression darkened to the point he hardly recognized her. She took a step back and crossed her arms. "Mess, huh? You honestly think of your own dad having had a stroke so callously?"

"Come on, Mill, it was just an expression. I didn't—"

"Hush." For what felt like eternity, she stood hugging herself, lips pressed tight, eyes luminous from tears threatening to spill. "For a second I actually felt sorry for you." She laughed before conking her forehead with her palm. "But now I realize who I'm dealing with—the guy your brother called *Cold Coop,* aka The Human Iceberg. Jim hated you for leaving like you did, but I always made excuses. I told him you were hurting. When our daughter was born, and you couldn't be bothered to meet her, I told him you were an integral part of our country's security, and that I was sure you'd come just as soon as you got leave. When our son was born, and you still didn't show…" She shook her head and chuckled. "Despite the fact that Peg had told you our happy news on the phone, I assured Jim you must not have received the official birth announcement, otherwise nothing could've kept you away. When Jim died, and you still didn't come home, well, that I chalked up to you being wrapped up in your own grief. But how could you bear knowing all of us were here falling

apart? How could you just carry on as if your brother and niece and nephew and father didn't even matter?"

By this time, Cooper had fully regained his emotions, while Millie seemed to be teetering on the edge. She didn't bother hiding her tears, and as usual, according to her capsulated version of the past decade and then some, he didn't bother to care. He sure didn't extend one iota of effort to provide her the comfort she obviously not only needed, but also deserved.

The woman was a saint, but after his meltdown, he felt empty inside. Like a shell. And so he just stood there. Stoic and still as if she'd been a drill sergeant giving him hell for not shining his shoes.

"What's wrong with you?" she shrieked. "You're like a machine—only instead of working, someone flipped your *off* switch. Peg needed you! *I* needed you, but you weren't there!" When she stepped deep into his personal space, pummeling his chest, he stood there and took it. He deserved the worst she could dish out and then some.

"I'm sorry," he finally said. And he was. But what did he want him to do? Sure, he'd help with his dad and the ranch, but he had no means with which to magically repair their mutually broken past. "Really sorry."

"S-sorry?" She laughed through her tears then raised her hand to slap him, only he caught her wrist and pulled her close, instinct screaming at him to hold on to her and never let go. This woman was a lifeline to all he'd once held dear. Every bad thing she'd said about him had been true. He was the worst of the worst. Lower than pond scum. For the past twelve years, she'd carried his world, and he'd callously, cruelly let her.

That stopped now.

He had to get a grip. But to do that, he'd need her help.

"I hate you," she said into his chest while keeping such a tight grip on his T-shirt that it pulled against his back.

"I know…" *I hate me.* He kissed the crown of her head. "I'm sorry. So crazy, freakin' sorry. But I'm back, and everything's going to be okay. I promise." *With every breath of my being, I promise, Millie.*

"I want to believe you." She sagged against him until he held the bulk of her weight just to keep her from crumpling to the floor. "But…"

She didn't have to finish her sentence for him to know what she'd been about to say. That of course she wanted to believe him, but when it came to his family, he'd dropped the proverbial ball so many times, it'd shattered.

Chapter Five

"Mom? Are you alive?"

Millie cautiously opened her tear-swollen eyes to find her son standing at the head of her bed. Though J.J.'s expression read concerned, his red snowsuit and Power Ranger hat and gloves read Snow Day.

"Cool! Since you are alive, can I go build a fort?"

She groaned. "Honey, what time is it? And did you do your chores?" On weekends and any other time they didn't have school, the kids were in charge of egg collecting and cleaning the litter box—not that they often saw the orange tabby named Cheetah, who mostly preferred hiding behind the dining room's half-dead ficus.

"Me and LeeAnn tried doing chores, but Uncle Coop already did 'em."

She sat up in the bed. "Even the cat box?"

"Well…" J.J. dropped his gaze in the telltale sign of a fib. "Since he made breakfast for me and Lee and Grandpa, I bet he did that and checked on the chickens, too."

"Uh-huh…" She grabbed her robe from the foot of the bed, then slipped her feet out from under the covers and into house shoes. The home had been built in 1905, meaning the woodstove and a few space heaters were all they had for heat. On many mornings, she'd woken to air cold enough to see her breath. Thankfully, this wasn't one. "Come on," she said to her son after switching off the valiantly humming space heater then shrugging into her robe and cinching the belt. "Let's see what's going on."

"Okay—" J.J. took her hand "—but we'd have more fun if we just went outside and built a fort."

"Why's that?" she asked with trepidation. To say the previous night had been rocky would be the understatement of the century. She and Cooper's uncomfortable scene had ended with her dashing upstairs and slamming her door. Not only had she been saddened and infuriated by her brother-in-law, but the fact that she'd then sought comfort from him as well had all been too much to bear. For the first time in recent memory, she'd cried herself to sleep. But she didn't have time for such folly. She had Clint and her children to care for—not to mention this godforsaken ranch. Most winter mornings, she woke wishing herself a million miles away. Then came spring, and along with the first daffodils, up rose her indefatigable hope.

"Well—" on the way down the stairs, J.J. wiped his runny nose on his coat sleeve "—Lee's having a fight with Uncle Cooper, and Grandpa's been making a *lot* of scary noises."

Swell…

From the base of the stairs, raised voices could clearly be heard.

"Grandpa doesn't like you! Leave him alone!"

"Doesn't matter if he likes me or not. He just needs to quit being a stubborn old mule and eat."

Never had Millie more understood the meaning

of being careful what she wished for. She'd long believed Cooper's return would be the answer to her every prayer, but apparently, she couldn't have been more wrong.

She hastened her pace only to find herself in the middle of even more chaos than the night before.

Cooper sat calmly on the edge of his father's bed, doing an admirable job of trying to feed him what she guessed from the beige splatters dotting his quilts, the floor and walls was oatmeal. With each new spoonful, he used his good arm to swat at his son.

"Gwet aut!" Clint hollered.

Initially, the shock of his volume took Millie aback, but then the significance of what'd just happened sank in. "Clint, you spoke!" She approached the bed and gestured for Cooper to hand her the oatmeal bowl. "That was awesome. Your speech therapist will be thrilled."

"I'm happy for you, Grandpa!" J.J. hugged Clint's clean arm.

"See, Dad?" Cooper took a damp dishrag from the rolling tray table and wiped cereal clumps from his father's red flannel pajama top. "No matter how much you hate me being here, I'm technically good for you."

"Arggghh!"

"What?" Cooper prompted his father. "I didn't quite catch that. Mind repeating?"

"Mom, make him stop," LeeAnn begged from the foot of the bed.

"Aigh ate uuu!"

"Mom, *please...*"

"What's that, old man?" Cooper taunted. "You hate me? Good, because right about now, I'm not exactly feeling warm and fuzzy toward you." He tapped his temple. "Even after all this time, though I can rationalize in my head that what happened to Mom was an accident, in here—" he patted his chest "—the way you treated me—the way you made your pal, the sheriff, keep me from attending my own mother's funeral? What the hell? Who does that? The whole thing still keeps me up at night."

"Stop!" LeeAnn cried to Cooper. "I don't blame Grandpa for hating you! You're the devil!"

"Lee!" Millie set the bowl on the nightstand in favor of going to her daughter. "Honey, please take J.J. outside to gather the eggs and make sure the heat lamp's still on."

"But, Mom, I—"

"Lee, just go." Millie hated being short with the girl, but felt at least temporarily removing her kids from this toxic environment was best for all involved. Deep down, as tough as this father-son duel was to witness, she suspected it was doing them both good.

"Fine." LeeAnn held out her hand to her brother. "Come on, brat."

"You're a brat!"

"Both of you, knock it off!" Millie snapped. What a difference a day made. She'd grown accustomed to constant worry, but this added a whole new dimension to family fun.

When the kids were outside, Millie drew Cooper into the hall, shutting Clint's door behind her. "Look, I think I get what you've been trying to do with your dad—the whole tough-love routine—but maybe adding stress to an already difficult situation isn't the best course."

"I wasn't *trying* to do anything. I heard him banging around in there, and since you were still sleeping and your friend Lynette called and said because her car won't start, she won't be able to make it today, I figured I'd give you a hand. Turns out the old bastard didn't want breakfast, but to give me a hard time."

"Cooper... You belittling him makes me uncomfortable."

"Sorry." Outside, the wind howled. In the cramped hall, he paced, his expression every bit as tormented as the storm. "At the moment, his very existence isn't doing much for me."

"You don't mean that."

"No, I don't, but honestly?" His pinched expression broke her heart. No—what really broke her heart was the way so much time had passed, yet everything between father and son had not only stayed the same, but maybe even grown worse. "I've been here just shy of twenty-four hours and feel like I'm going batshit crazy. I know my dad's going through a rough patch, but we're all in this together now."

She winced at his language, though mirrored the sentiment.

"If you don't mind taking over in there—" he gestured toward his dad's room "—I need to check the cattle."

Though he was yet again retreating, Millie knew that this time it was only temporary and for a noble cause. Their prized herd did need to be checked, and the fact that she wouldn't be the one making the long ride out to the south pasture in these treacherous conditions made her heart swell with gratitude.

"Thank you."

"You're welcome." His gaze met hers and locked. His intensity startled her to the point that she had to look away. Her pulse raced, and she wasn't sure what to do with her hands, so she fussed with her robe's belt, feeling all of thirteen upon realizing that Cooper was still the most handsome cowboy in town. Don't get her wrong—she'd loved her husband with every ounce of her being, but Jim had been a kind soul. Cooper? Well, even back in high school his downright sinful sooty-lashed stare had made rodeo queens swoon and female teachers forgive missing homework.

From the kitchen came the sound of the back door crashing open. "Mom!" LeeAnn hollered. "Come quick!"

Covering her suddenly flushed face with her hands, Millie found herself actually welcoming whatever emergency her daughter had brought inside. At least it would distract her from Cooper's mossy-green gaze.

The rooster's crow coming from the kitchen was her first clue that she should abandon all hope of finding peace that morning.

"Mom, the heat lamp's not on and the chickens were shivering. We're bringing them inside."

Millie pressed her lips tight while J.J. set his favorite golden wyandotte on the kitchen floor. She fussed a bit, fluffing her feathers and preening, then made a beeline for the cat food.

Cooper cut her off at the pass to set the food bowl on the counter. "Mill, before we get the house full of feathers and chicken shit, do you have a spare bulb for the lamp in case it's an easy fix?"

J.J. gaped. "Uncle Cooper, you're not allowed to say that word."

"Sorry." He had the good grace to actually redden.

"Apology accepted." Millie was embarrassed to

admit she didn't have spare anything. The bulbs had been on her shopping list for ages, but with barely enough money to pay for food, let alone heat, what was the point of even having a list? "And no, I don't have an extra."

"Okay…" He covered his face with his hands, then sighed. "J.J., how about you help your mom build some kind of pen, and I'll help your sister bring the chickens inside—"

LeeAnn shuffled through the back door, carrying a hen under each arm. "It's freezing out there, and a branch knocked a hole in the roof."

Millie groaned, looking heavenward to ask, "Really? Our plates aren't already full enough?"

"Relax." Behind her, Cooper lightly rubbed her shoulders. "We'll keep the chickens inside until the storm passes, then, after our next supply run, I'll rig a lamp for them in one of the empty horse stalls in the barn. Hopefully, the coop shouldn't take but a day or two to fix."

"Sure. Thanks." She didn't want to find comfort in his take-charge demeanor and especially not from his touch, but how could she not when it felt as if she'd been running uphill ever since Clint's stroke? To now have a man around to do the stereotypically manly chores made her feel as if her uphill charge had, at least for the time being, transitioned to a stroll through a nice, flat meadow. Call her old-fashioned, but when it came to gender roles, she missed doing mostly so-called woman's work. "J.J., hon, do me a favor and run out to get some firewood. Pretend it's giant Lincoln Logs and build a little fence."

"Cool! That sounds fun!" He dashed outside.

LeeAnn had placed the ladder-backed table chairs in front of the living room and hall pass-throughs. She was such a good girl. Always eager to help. It broke Millie's heart to see her always so blue—even more so ever since Cooper had shown up. Would she eventually cut him some slack?

Millie glanced his way to find him bundled up, once again wearing Jim's duster. He'd slapped his hat on, and the mere sight of him took her breath away. She wanted to stay mad at him for having left all those years ago, but she lacked the energy to fight.

"I'll bring in the rest of the hens then check on the cattle."

"Thank you," she said to him, then again to her daughter, who'd cleaned poo with a damp paper towel.

Cold air lingered when Cooper left. It smelled crisp and clean. Of cautious hope.

"He's awful," LeeAnn said after Cooper had closed the door. "I wish he'd stayed away."

"I'm sorry about what you saw between him and Grandpa. When your grandma died, things were…" Where did she start in explaining to her little girl just how terrible Clint's grief had actually been? True, what'd happened to Kay had been an accident, but Clint had treated his elder son as if the tragedy had been no less than murder. The uglier details weren't the sort of matter she cared to casually discuss with her daughter. "Well… Things were really hard. And Grandpa and your uncle… They didn't get along. Your uncle didn't leave because he wanted to, but because Grandpa made him."

LeeAnn furrowed her brows. "Grandpa Clint wouldn't do that. He's nice."

"Sure, he is. But, honey, remember that this all happened a long time ago. Way before you were even born. Your uncle has a right to be upset. So does Grandpa. The two of them have a lot of talking to do, but that's kind of hard with Grandpa not being able to talk." Millie would be lying if she didn't admit to also harboring a deep well of resentment toward her husband's brother. But acting on that now wouldn't get the chickens in from the cold or make sure the cattle were okay or perform Clint's morning bathing routine.

"Mom?" LeeAnn picked up a chicken, stroking her neck until the creature happily cooed. Millie thought it was Cluck—the kids had them all named, but she couldn't keep them straight. "Do you still miss Daddy?"

The question caught Millie off guard and raised a lump in her throat. "Of course. I think about him every day."

"Good." She set down the chicken to hug Millie. "I didn't like it when Uncle Cooper rubbed your shoulders the way Daddy used to. My friend Julie's mom and dad got divorced, and now her mom married some new guy who Julie doesn't like. I don't want you to be with anyone else."

"Honey, where is all of this coming from?" Millie tipped up LeeAnn's chin, searching her dear features. "Your father meant the world to me. He always will."

"Promise?"

Millie had just nodded when J.J. and Cooper laughed their way through the back door. Both carried squawking hens and were red-cheeked and coated in a dusting of snow. The vision of her smiley son warmed her more efficiently than a roaring fire. As for the fire in her belly Cooper's whisker-stubbled jaw evoked, well, she just wasn't going there.

"You should see it, Mom!" J.J.'s nose ran, so she handed him a paper towel to use to wipe it. "That tree smooshed the chicken coop like Godzilla! *Bam! Rwaar!*"

"It's that bad?" she asked Cooper.

"'Fraid so." His expression was grim. "It's a wonder none of the *occupants* were hurt."

A series of muffled growls erupted from Clint's room.

Millie punctuated those with her own groan.

"Want me to check on him?" Cooper offered.

"Thanks, but the mom in me thinks you two should be grounded from each other."

Judging by Cooper's scowl, he disagreed with her judgment. "Whatever. J.J.? Wanna check the cattle with me?"

"Yeah!" His supersize grin faded. "But I need to build the chicken fence first. Can you wait?"

"I'll do you one better—while you work on the fence, I'll grab some plywood and straw from the barn. We'll use it to protect your mom's floor until we rig a heat lamp in the barn."

"Okay!" J.J. dashed outside for more wood.

"Cooper…" Millie's mind reeled. Too much was happening too fast. LeeAnn making her promise to never love another man besides Jim. Chickens in her kitchen. J.J.'s instant connection with his uncle. LeeAnn's instant hatred of him. Toss Clint and way too much snow into the mix and Millie's plate wasn't just full, but spilling over onto her now filthy kitchen floor. "Do you think it's wise to take J.J. out to check the cattle?"

"Why wouldn't it be? He's already bundled up. I assume he can ride?"

"Well, sure. Jim had him on horseback practically since he learned to walk."

Cooper sighed. "Then what's the problem?"

Where did she start? Her son was beyond precious to her. Along with his sister, the duo had been her reason for living ever since Jim died. As much as one part of her appreciated Cooper riding in on his white horse disguised as a ratty old pickup, another part of her resented his very presence. She and Clint had managed on their own for all these years and didn't need Cooper showing up, thinking he had all the answers. Only the joke was on her, because at the moment, as overwhelmed as she was—he did.

A fact that scared her to her core.

Because Cooper might be a dependable, stand-up guy in the Navy. But when it came to his track record on being around when his family needed him most? His stats were an abysmal 1-288-0. A single, early-morning chicken rescue hardly made him a trustworthy man.

Chapter Six

Cooper gritted his teeth against the icy assault that had him pulling his hat brim lower and his coat collar higher. Clouds may have cleared, making way for blinding sun, but the wind had only grown stronger, driving the dry twelve inches of snow into an otherworldly landscape of towering drifts and bare earth.

"Sorry, girl." He leaned forward, stroking Sassy's mane.

It was a good thing he hadn't dragged his nephew out here—though if the kid planned on making his living off the land he would soon enough have to learn how much fun it was working in less than ideal conditions.

Cooper would've given his left nut for his SEAL cold-weather gear right about now. He was a damn fool for thinking Jim's duster and his straw hat could handle what had to be a wind chill well into negative digits.

A thirty-minute ride landed him in the heart of the herd. They'd strayed a good mile from the feed station, so after driving them all in that direction, he broke the stock tank's ice, then headed back to the barn.

With the wind at his back, the trek wasn't quite as miserable, but damn near close.

He got Sassy settled in her stall then loaded his truck

bed with hay bales and range cubes before heading back out to the herd. He considered himself a die-hard traditionalist, much preferring to check cattle on horseback, but years and missions had battered his body, and the cold combined with being back in a saddle made him ache in places he'd forgotten he had.

With the heater blasting and staticky Hank Williams playing on the radio, Cooper's mind was no longer preoccupied with the cold, but considering he now had the luxury of allowing his mind to wander while zigzagging between drifts, that wasn't necessarily a good thing.

When he refused to think about his cantankerous old man, or the laser beams of hate his niece blasted him with, his thoughts drifted to the forbidden—Millie in her robe. The way it'd hung open at her throat, showing far too much collarbone than he'd been comfortable seeing.

He'd always had a thing for that particular spot on a woman. But Millie wasn't just any woman. Their shared history made his most complex missions look like a cakewalk. She'd been his brother's wife, for God's sake. Some things were sacred between brothers and that was one. *Thou shall not covet thy brother's wife.*

Didn't matter that Jim was long gone.

It was a matter of principle.

Cooper had thankfully reached the herd, squelching the whole issue by busting up hay bales then spreading range cubes. Bellows and snorts accompanied his surprisingly satisfying work.

Though Cooper was usually outside, he couldn't remember the last time he'd been around animals. He'd missed it. The work's simple grace. No one shot at him. No one's life was at stake if he forgot any of a mission's minutiae. Don't get him wrong—he loved his job, but this…

He breathed deeply of the lung-searing cold air, but instead of it bothering him, he found it invigorating. He hadn't realized how much he'd missed this place. How much this land was still a part of him.

Like Millie?

Yeah… He wasn't going there.

He finished counting cattle, only to come up one short of the seventy-six Peg had told him they had.

Shit.

Considering that this stretch of the family land was pancake flat for as far as the eye could see, and the Black Angus contrasted sharply against the winter grass and snow, this meant the stray was hidden behind a drift, either lost or hurt.

It took an hour of meandering through the drifts, but he finally found her, only to have his stomach knot with concern. Why hadn't Millie or Peg told him they had a momma due to deliver a winter calf? Never failed, they always somehow managed to come in a storm.

The cow had found a slight dip in the land, and in the few minutes he'd been watching, she'd already gotten up and down only to get back up again. Judging by the half-frozen fluid on her hind legs, her water sack had recently broken, only her teats were slick and shiny— usually an indication that she'd already had her calf and it had fed. Most cows safely delivered their calves without incident, and they usually didn't appreciate a crowd. Judging by the momma's level of agitation, it looked like this was the case here.

Despite this fact, with the temps so low, he'd feel a

lot better at least seeing the calf to make sure it seemed healthy.

He approached the cow nice and slow, only to get a surprise. "I'll be damned…" Tucked in between drifts was one cleaned, contented-looking calf and another looking forlorn and shivering. "Looks like someone had twins."

Didn't happen often, but when it did, one of the calves ran the risk of being rejected.

Cooper removed his coat, wrapped it around the shivering calf, then settled it in the truck bed. His hope was that the cow would see her calf and follow with the other, but no such luck. Just as he'd feared, she'd rejected her second born, which meant it would be up to Cooper to bottle feed it milk and colostrum.

Back when he'd helped out on a daily basis, Cooper remembered Clint having kept some frozen—just in case. If not, Cooper would put in a call to the vet.

He looked back to find the cow's firstborn on her feet and nursing—a great sign that all was well where they were concerned. But the little one he moved to the truck's front seat wasn't yet out of the woods.

"Let's get you warmed up."

The poor little thing still shivered.

Cooper revved the engine, then turned the heater knob to high.

Since he knew the way through the snowdrift maze, the trip to the barn took under ten minutes—only now that the calf had stopped shivering, Cooper was reluctant to put the little darlin' back outside without a heat lamp.

What would Millie say about having chickens and a calf in her kitchen? The thought of her pretty face all scrunched into a frown made him smile. But what really warmed him through and through was the certainty that even though she might temporarily be caught off guard by their houseguest, she'd care for it as well as she did every other creature in the house.

He admired the hell out of her. She understandably didn't think much of him. Would that ever change? Would she ever again think of herself not just as his sister-in-law, but as his friend?

"SORRY, PEG, BUT I've gotta go." Millie pressed the off button on the phone then stared at Cooper and what he'd brought through the back door. "*Really?* Helga couldn't have held on a little longer?" For a split second, Millie indulged in feeling sorry for herself at having a calf added to her kitchen menagerie, but then she surged into action. The only guarantee her life had ever come with was that what could go wrong, would. This was just another one of those occasions.

"Helga?" Cooper shifted his weight from one leg to the other. The calf was woefully small, but Millie guessed him to still weigh between sixty and seventy pounds. "You couldn't have come up with a better name?"

"Cool!" J.J. bounded into the kitchen. "Does this mean we have a pet cow?"

"Only until we get a heating lamp rigged in the barn." Millie tugged Cooper by his coat sleeve to follow her onto the heated back porch. She fit the drain plug in the oversize utility sink, then ran warm water. "Let's get him clean and warmed up."

Cooper gingerly nestled the calf into the big sink.

It was a tight squeeze—probably the bathtub would've been a better fit—but for now, this would do.

What wouldn't do? The awkward awareness stemming from working alongside Cooper—especially when every so often his elbow accidentally grazed her breasts. In an effort to keep her mind on the calf's welfare, as opposed to her jittery hands and inability to even hold the mild pet shampoo, she asked, "I'm assuming the little guy's momma rejected him. Got any clue why?"

"*Helga* had twins. Her firstborn's fat and happy. My guess is she was as surprised by this one as we are."

"Twins… Never saw that coming." With her hands sudsy, Millie nudged hair from her cheek with her shoulder, but that only landed the escaped curl on her mouth.

"Let me help…" Cooper swept the lock over her cheek, tucking it behind her ear. His finger was warm and wet and blazed a trail she could feel, but didn't want to.

"Thanks—not just for that, but you know…bringing in this guy."

He nodded, but then graced her with a slow grin that did funny things to her stomach. "No problem. I'm not a total deadbeat, you know."

"Yeah…" *I do.*

Time slowed as she drank him in, remembering the many good times she and Jim and Cooper had shared. But she couldn't just flip a switch and make all those years she'd hated and resented him for not being there go away. Even before they'd been in-laws, they'd been friends. Good, lifelong friends. She'd never known her dad, and her mom had virtually abandoned her to be raised by her maternal grandparents. The Hansens had been like a second family to her. It'd been inconceivable how Cooper had lived with himself for not having come home.

But he's home now. Shouldn't that count for something?

"Dad still keep colostrum in the deep freeze?"

"There should be some in there."

"Good. When we finish, I'll make a bottle."

"Thanks. I'll find you the powdered formula."

"I'd appreciate it."

What changed? Why the stilted formality?

She finished scrubbing the calf then let the water drain before rinsing him with the sprayer. Under Cooper's appraisal, her every movement felt stiff and labored—as if she were under water.

A growl followed by metallic clanking came from the general direction of Clint's room.

"Want me to check on Grandpa?" The whole time Millie had stood hyperaware of Cooper, LeeAnn and J.J. had hovered near the kitchen pass-through. What did that say about her state of mind that she hadn't even noticed her kids had been in the room?

"I'll do it," she said.

Cooper asked, "What do you want me to do about this guy?"

"Lee, please grab a couple of old quilts—you know, the ones I put over the garden for frost?"

The girl nodded.

"Pile them in the corner by the fridge. It should be nice and warm."

"Yes, ma'am."

"J.J.—" Millie knelt to his level "—I need you to run down to the basement and get the feeder bottles we used when we had those two calves with scours. They should be somewhere on the shelves by my flowerpots."

"Okay." Her son bit his lower lip while his eyes filled with tears. "Is the baby going to be all right? He's so tiny."

She pulled J.J. into a hug. Her son had already witnessed too many hardships during his short life. She couldn't bear for him to have one more. "He will if I have anything to say about it."

WITH THE CALF nestled in a cozy quilt nest, Cooper ducked his head while taking the ninety-degree turn on the basement stairs. He'd conked his head on the damned rafter so many times as a gangly teen that even his long absence couldn't make him forget.

J.J. clomped behind him as they descended into the cool, damp cavernous space. "Did you know my dad?"

"Sure did." Cooper swept aside a low-hanging cobweb.

"Are you like him?"

Not really. Jim had always been the better of the two of them. Kinder. The sort who volunteered to stay home from a weekend bender to help an elderly neighbor plant her garden. "I suppose we looked a little alike. He was my brother."

"Like Lee's my sister?"

"Right." Cooper opened the freezer lid, welcoming the blast of cold air on his heated cheeks. Made him uncomfortable thinking about what a selfish prick he used to be.

The kid took a scooter that'd been leaned against a wall and rode it across the stone floor. "I'd rather have a brother. Lee's grumpy all the time. And did you know she talks to *boys?*"

Cooper looked up from the freezer. "How old is she?"

"She's in fifth grade. My friend Cayden said he saw her kiss a kid who's in sixth grade. Isn't that gross?"

Actually, yes.

Just a guess, but Cooper didn't think his brother would be on board with this kind of information. As the girl's uncle, had he been there for her since Jim's death, Cooper would've felt right at home giving her a stern lecture on staying the hell away from boys until she was thirty.

"Do you know what sex is? Cayden said his biggest brother got caught having sex on their couch."

Though Cooper already had the colostrum, he stuck his head back in the chest-style freezer just to escape the kid's questioning stare.

"Well?" J.J. unfortunately persisted. "Do you know what sex is?"

Cooper coughed. What kind of kids was Millie raising? "Actually, I do know what it is—bad. Very, very bad, and it's not anything you need to be talking about till you're thirty." *Would that fall under the* do as I say, not as I do *form of parenting?* Cooper lost his virginity at sixteen to a nineteen-year-old dental hygienist in the bed of her truck.

"Oh." J.J. stopped riding. "Okay, well, I won't do it, then."

"Excellent. Glad to hear it."

"Do you remember what I was s'posed to be getting?"

"These?" Cooper had spied three plastic feeder bottles exactly where Millie had described and grabbed them.

"Yeah! Bottles!"

Eager to not only escape the gloomy basement, but also his nephew's questions, Cooper headed back up the stairs, figuring the kid would follow. Only he didn't. "Aren't you coming?"

"Do you want me to?"

"I guess." Cooper furrowed his eyebrows. What did that mean? Was this some kind of trick question? "I mean, your mom told you to help, right?"

He nodded.

"Okay, then, come on…" He pressed against the wall, urging J.J. to pass him on the stairs.

"Cool!" The kid bolted as if he was on springs. "Do you think the calf's gonna live or die like my dad?"

Cooper inwardly groaned. If having rugrats always involved this many awkward questions, he wanted no part of ever having a child of his own.

Chapter Seven

By the time the kids had been put to bed and Clint's evening care had been completed, Millie collapsed onto the sofa, setting the baby monitor she used to make sure he didn't need her in the night on the coffee table. Every inch of her ached from the exertion of their action-packed day.

Cheetah, the cat, slinked out from behind the recliner to dart into the kitchen.

"I don't even know why I feed you," she said to the inhospitable creature.

When the phone rang, she contemplated letting the machine pick up, but on the chance it was one of Clint's home-health therapists, she mustered the energy to fish the phone from the couch cushions—the spot where LeeAnn typically left it. "Hello?"

"Well? How's it going? You were supposed to call me back."

Peg. Millie had forgotten she'd been on the phone with Cooper's sister right before he'd shown up with the calf.

"What happened?"

Since the upstairs shower was still running, Millie

gave her sister-in-law the short version of the chaotic day's events.

"Wait—so why do you still have a calf and chickens in the kitchen?"

"Because of the storm, the feed store had a run on heat-lamp bulbs. Ernest won't have more in till he can make a supply run to Denver."

"Good grief." Peg groaned. "I'm working twelve-hour shifts, so I can have long weekends off. Want me to pick one up for you before I head your way?"

"Thanks for the offer, but the even worse news is that one of the biggest limbs on the cottonwood out back fell on the coop. It's a total loss. Your brother said he can rebuild it, but who knows how long that'll take."

"You can't have chickens in your house indefinitely...."

"I know..." Millie drew the afghan from the sofa back to tuck it around her legs. "Cooper's rigging a temporary fix in the barn. Since the kids have school tomorrow, we're driving into Denver for the parts he needs."

"Who's staying with Dad?"

"Lynette. Plus, the traveling nurse should be here." After they found chicken-coop supplies, they'd grocery shop.

"Good. You need a break."

"Agreed. Only..." She wrapped one of the afghan's frayed strands around her pinkie finger tight enough for her nail to turn white.

"What's the problem?"

Upstairs, the shower turned off.

The thought of Cooper standing there buck naked struck her as disconcerting. The old house only had one and a half baths, meaning...

Her cheeks flamed.

"The problem," she said to her sister-in-law in an effort to get her wandering mind back on topic, "is your
brother. He's everywhere. I can't think around him.
He's just—"

Back on her feet, she fished behind a row of Jim's
dusty old civil war history tomes for the Oreos she kept
hidden in a Ziploc bag. It wasn't that she begrudged the
kids' cookies—she made them all the time. But Oreos
were her thing. Her grandmother had always laughed
about the baking gene having skipped her generation.
She'd filled their cookie jar with store-bought fare. Millie hadn't complained. All these years later, the same
treat that'd gotten her through her rocky early childhood
was still her go-to food security blanket.

A creak on the stairs had her chewing faster, before
tucking the bag back in its hiding place.

"What're you stashing?"

Hand to her chest, she willed her racing pulse to slow.
"Cooper. You scared me half to death."

"Good thing it was only halfway," he teased without smiling.

"Yeah…" Back in school, they used to be friends,
so why now did she find herself wishing he'd just stay
in his room?

From the phone she'd cradled between her breasts,
Peg's tinny voice asked, "Millie? Millie, are you there?"

"That my sister?"

She nodded.

He reached for the phone.

During the hand-off, their fingers brushed, which
only flustered her further. What was it about him that
had her feeling like she'd returned to seventh grade?

"Hey, girl. When do I get to see you?"

Cheetah returned to do a figure-eight around Cooper's ankles. *Traitor.*

While Cooper and his sister talked, Millie checked to make sure Clint's meds had kicked in then wandered into the kitchen with the intent to unload the dishwasher. But when she flicked on the lights, it woke the menagerie, and the rooster quite literally flew his makeshift coop. Having always considered herself a reasonably intelligent person, why hadn't she thought earlier about devising a way to keep her flock from flying?

She'd hoped catching Barry would be easy, but he'd landed atop the fridge.

"When I do catch you," she said in a singsong voice while easing one of the kitchen table chairs in his direction, "I'm going to fry you."

She stood on the chair, slowly reaching for the stupid bird.

"Need help?"

Upon hearing Cooper's voice, Barry was back on the move, finally resting on the rim of LeeAnn's lopsided volcano that she'd left on the table.

"I nearly had him, if you'd stop skulking."

"Skulking?" He crept toward the bird, and in a ridiculously fast move, had him captured and tucked under his arm.

"You know what I mean." What a mess. Everything was just such an awful mess—and she wasn't just talking about her kitchen, which would have to be fumigated once the chickens and calf got to their temporary home in the barn. She feared the truest source of disarray was her own heart. Having her brother-in-law back in the mix was all at once a godsend and a curse. "You're always so sneaky."

"Mill..." He stroked the side of the bird's head. And damn Barry for closing his eyes and cooing. "All I did was walk into the room. No sneaking or skulking. Just walking." He took the phone from the waistband of his black warm-up pants, returning it to the charging stand.

Whatever! Just stop!

Like a doofus, she still stood on the chair in front of the fridge and stared at him. Mouth dry, pulse haywire, she felt on the edge of a breakdown and had no idea why! His being there should've made everything easier. He'd certainly lightened her workload. So why did everything suddenly seem so hard?

Maybe because he wore no shirt, and his chest and abs formed a muscular wall?

"Need help?" he asked.

"With what?" Flighty hand to her mouth, she nibbled the tip of her pinkie finger.

"Getting down? Wiping all those Oreo crumbs off your T-shirt? Rigging something to keep old Barry here from another flight?"

"H-how do you know his name?"

"Your son told me. He's a good kid."

"The best." Why was her mouth so dry? Why did her right eye keep twitching every time she looked Cooper's way? And how did he know she'd been eating Oreos? And why did just thinking about him looking at her chest cause her nipples to harden? Lord, she was a bona fide Texas twister of a disaster!

"Help?" He now stood beside her. Even with the benefit of her chair, she was only a few inches taller.

"Thanks, but I can do it." After scrambling down,

she shoved the chair back under the table then brushed crumbs from her chest.

He took a step back, raising his hands in surrender. "Want me to handle tucking in our escapee?"

"W-would you mind?" Because honestly, after their hectic day, Millie had more than she could handle with just being in the same close space as Cooper. "I—I'm ready for bed."

She retrieved Clint's monitor from the living room then made her own escape up the stairs.

The dimly lit kitchen was too intimate.

It brought back memories of all the nights she and Jim sat at the table over cups of steaming cocoa, plotting and planning the rest of their lives. Whether to sign J.J. up for baseball or steer him toward rodeo. Whether they should let LeeAnn enroll in that hoity-toity Denver art class her second-grade teacher had recommended. When Jim had been alive, everything had seemed so simple. He and Clint ran the ranch, and she cared for them, their children and home.

Now?

She wore so many hats that if she sprouted eight extra heads, she still couldn't wear them all.

After brushing her teeth in the bathroom, which still smelled rich from Cooper's musky shampoo, she checked on J.J. to find him sleeping.

She took the toy truck out from under his flannel pajama-clad legs then tugged the covers up to his chin. She kissed his forehead, whispering, "I love you."

From behind LeeAnn's door came a girly giggle. *"You're crazy..."*

Millie didn't bother knocking, and upon entering the

room, she held out her hand. She and her daughter had done this dance before. "Phone."

LeeAnn sighed with majestic preteen aplomb. "God, Mom, I'm almost twelve, and everyone on the planet has a cell but me."

"Gosh, Lee, you may be right, but that doesn't give you permission to take my cell from my purse. You know we only have it for emergencies, and those minutes are expensive."

"I hate you, and I hate being poor!" Back in bed, her daughter finished her performance by tugging the covers over her head.

This probably should've been the moment when Millie nipped that sass by grounding LeeAnn for the rest of her life, but she didn't have the strength. After perching on the bed's edge, she ran her hand along her daughter's side. "Know what? I'm kind of sick of being poor myself, only you might find this hard to believe, but hon, we're actually pretty rich—and blessed. We have a nice, solid roof over our heads and plenty of food in our bellies. We have each other and love and—"

"Stop!" LeeAnn sat up, letting the quilts fall around her waist. "You say we're so rich and blessed? Then how come Daddy died and Grandpa had a stroke? And our barn's so crappy that the chickens have to live in our kitchen?"

"Lee..." Millie's throat tightened. She'd asked herself the same questions countless times, and was fresh out of fortifying platitudes. "Look, since you're *sooo* old, I'll be straight with you. No one's more tired of our temporary cash *shortage* than me, but it is what it is. I wasn't raised to be a quitter and neither were you.

When times are tough, we just have to dig in our heels and fight harder. We—"

"Mom, seriously, *please* stop. Our life sucks. Everything sucks, and sometimes I just want to run away!" She was crying, and the sound of her child's sobs shattered what little remained of Millie's heart.

"Okay, yes—" she drew LeeAnn into a hug "—at the moment, there's not a whole lot to be happy about, but you know what?"

"What?" Sniff, sniff.

"On the bright side, things can't get much worse, right?"

Millie kissed the crown of her daughter's head, then tucked her in, longing for simpler times back when Jim had been here to coparent. J.J. she could still handle, but with her daughter, Millie felt about as in control as if she were juggling boiling water.

In the hall, she'd just shut LeeAnn's door and turned for her own room when Cooper reached the top of the stairs.

When their eyes locked, she stopped breathing.

Had she really just noted that things couldn't get worse?

"Everything all right?" he asked.

She wagged the cell. "Just putting on my sheriff hat. Guess I'm not ready for her to be acting this old so soon. When we were her age, no one had phones."

"True. But then to her way of thinking, we probably seem old enough to have been riding dinosaurs to school." He cracked a smile. "Pretty sure your old Chevette could've technically been from the Stone Age. That thing was nasty."

"Oh—" she raised her eyebrows "—like your truck was much better?"

"At least it was a Ford."

"Watch it…" Lord, Cooper and Jim used to battle for hours over the merits of Ford versus Chevy trucks. She'd forgotten. In the hall's chill, her throat knotted under the guilty weight of how much else of her husband's daily quirks she'd forgotten.

Outside, the wind had once again picked up and rattled the shutters.

"I really am sorry about Jim. I would've come to the funeral, but didn't even know he'd died until a month after he'd been gone. By then…" He shrugged. Rammed his hands into his pockets. "Well, I couldn't."

"Sure. I understand." But she didn't. Which was no doubt a big part of the reason why she found it so difficult being around him.

COOPER HID OUT from Millie until she'd shut herself into her room for the night.

Once the coast was clear, he handled the half-dozen chores still needing to be addressed, then was too keyed up to sleep. He tried boning up on the latest deep-dive recs, but his job felt a million miles away. What he really needed to think about, but didn't want to, was the mess he'd made of things here.

He sat on the sofa, leaning forward to cradle his forehead in his hands.

In the short run, he'd soon enough get the ranch in ship-shape order, but what about long-term? Would Millie and he ever again be on friendly terms? Would he grow as close to his niece and nephew as an uncle rightfully should?

Then there was Clint…

Cooper rose, heading toward his father's room, careful to avoid the creakiest spots in the old wood floor.

In the moonlight, his dad looked frail. His breathing was labored, and the cantankerous old goat had worked off all of his covers.

Quietly and efficiently, Cooper straightened Clint's linens, tucking them in hopes that they'd stay put through the night.

His feelings where his dad was concerned were all over the map. Of course Cooper loved him, but that love was tainted by the alienation Clint had caused. But then was it fair to blame his father for their estrangement, when if Cooper hadn't hurt his mother, nothing in any of their lives would've even changed?

MILLIE WOKE EARLIER than she would've liked. At five-thirty, it was still dark and the wind still blew. Not up to dealing with chickens and the calf in her robe, she pulled on jeans and a hoodie, topping her thick socks with her most comfortable pair of pink cowboy boots.

Jim had bought them for her as a first wedding anniversary present. She'd been so proud. They were decadent and impractical, and she still loved them as much as she did him. Only he was long gone, and over the years she'd found her remembered love changing. Sometimes, she loved him as a wife. Other times, almost in a mothering capacity when she wished she could scold him for having been so reckless with his precious life. Like his mom, he hadn't had to die. If she'd stayed on the porch. If he'd stayed in his seat, both would've still been alive today.

In the kitchen, she was surprised to find a few much-needed fortifications to their makeshift pens. Hay bales now formed a sturdier wall for the chickens, and a tent had been made from purple-striped disposable table-cloths left over from LeeAnn's last birthday. She peeked under to find Barry and his harem still sleeping.

"How are you?" she asked the tiny calf, stroking the top of his soft head.

He also had a new hay bale enclosure, and while the width made the kitchen feel smaller, she was glad to know there wouldn't soon be a stampede.

When had Cooper done all of this? He'd never been so conscientious as a teen.

"You probably need a bottle, huh? It's been a while since your last feeding." For optimum health, he'd need to be fed every twelve hours for the next three months. How many changes would've happened by then? Would Clint be walking or talking? Would the new chicken coop be done? Would she feel comfortable being in the same space as her brother-in-law? "Hard to believe it'll be almost Easter when we get you back with the herd."

He looked up at her with his big, dark eyes, and she melted.

"How could your mother not love you?"

She rubbed his nose, smiling when his warm exhalations tickled her palm.

By the time she finished warming the calf's milk and feeding him his bottle, the chickens were waking with throaty gurgles. She was just about to launch a search for feed in the coop's ruin when she noticed the bag leaning against the wall. The scoop was even inside.

Cooper had thought of everything. Right down to bringing in the water and feeder bowls—she'd made do with a paper plate and plastic mixing bowl.

She should be grateful toward him, so why the flash of resentment?

Since Clint's stroke, she'd single-handedly cared for the house and ranch. In her head she knew her brother-in-law was a godsend, but her heart told another story. For her, his mere presence was an admission that she couldn't cope. Which honestly? Okay, was true. But her stubborn streak didn't want to admit it—especially to of all people, Cooper.

Scowling, she bypassed coffee in favor of her private cookie stash.

In the dark living room, guided by moonlight reflecting off snow, she took her bag to the sofa. Only just as she was about to sit, something beneath the afghan moved!

Chapter Eight

"Unless you want things to get awkward real fast," Cooper said from the sofa, "you might want to sit somewhere else."

"There you go again…" Breathing heavy, Millie clutched her cookie bag to her chest. In the pale moonlight, she looked fragile. Still pretty, but dangerously thin and pale. "Skulking."

Groaning, he rubbed his hands over his whisker-stubbled face. "You try sitting on me, and yet I'm the bad guy?"

"I didn't say—" she dropped one of her contraband half-eaten cookies back in the bag "—never mind. What're you even doing here? Why weren't you sleeping in your old room?"

"Funny…" He eased upright. It'd been a long time since he'd done manual labor, and his body felt every hay bale and feed sack he'd lifted. Back on base, he worked out religiously, but lifting weights and swimming had nothing on the whole ranch routine. He felt every one of his thirty years and then some. "Ever since setting foot back on this land, I've worked my ass off to make things easier on you, but all you've done is complain. If you don't want me here, why did you ask me to come?"

"Point of fact?" She sat on his dad's recliner, but far from leaning back to relax, she remained as straight and unwelcoming as a fence post. "I wasn't the one asking you to come home. That was your sister."

"Want me to leave?"

Yes! "No. Of course not. I just... Well, maybe we could establish a few ground rules as to where you'll be and when?"

"Ground rules?" Had she lost her ever-lovin' mind? "As in, I shouldn't leave my room between the hours of 6:00 p.m and 6:00 a.m.?"

"Exactly." He'd meant the question to be sarcastic, but judging by her eager nod, she'd totally missed his point. "The less time you spend with the kids and me, the better. I thought we could somehow recapture our old *happy family* vibe, but..." She shook her head. "Your dad's expected to make a full recovery, so once he's back on his horse, you should—"

"Climb back on mine and ride the hell out of town?"

She blanched. "I didn't mean it like that."

He leaned forward, resting his elbows on his knees. "I'll bite. Go ahead, Mill, explain to me how else you—"

"Mommy?"

Cooper glanced over his shoulder to find sleepy, messy-haired J.J. The kid was crazy cute. Smart. Jim would be damned proud.

"Hey, hon." She went to her son, pulling him against her for a hug. "You're up early."

"I know. I was excited to see if we have another snow day."

"Gosh, I forgot to check. Let's turn on the TV and see."

She scooped up her little boy and carried him to the recliner, settling him on her lap.

J.J. took the remote from a side table and soon had the room filled with a cooking segment on making snow ice cream. School closings scrolled across the bottom of the screen.

How many mornings had Cooper sat in that same chair, holding his breath with his fingers crossed to see Wilmington Public Schools.

The scroll restarted with the statement that *Aurora Public Schools will be in session.* Wilmington hadn't been listed.

"Aw, man…" Wearing a mighty pout, J.J. crossed his arms. "I wanted to help build the new chicken coop."

"Trust me," Cooper said, "probably for the next week or even two, I'll need plenty of help."

"Okay…" He scrambled from his mom's lap. "Guess I'll eat cereal and pet the calf."

"Sounds like a great plan," Millie said.

"I like him…" Cooper hadn't meant to give the thought voice, and now that he had, in light of his sister-in-law flat out telling him she didn't want him being around her kids, he couldn't figure out why. What would forging a relationship with them hurt? Especially with their father gone.

He looked up to find Millie staring.

For a split second, their gazes locked, but then she turned away. "Think about what I said. I don't mean you should literally stay in your room whenever the kids are home, but you might think about heading out to the barn or maybe looking up old friends."

When a clang and growl erupted from his father's room, Millie bolted toward that direction.

Cooper leaned forward, cradling his face in his hands. Why was he even here? He wasn't wanted.

But you are clearly needed.

For now, that would have to be enough. He'd spent his entire adult life helping others in need, and he wasn't about to stop now—no matter what Millie said.

"RELAX. CLINT WILL be fine."

Millie hugged her longtime friend and neighbor, Lynette, whispering in her ear, "It's not him I'm worried about. How am I going to last an entire day being alone with Cooper?"

After checking to make sure Cooper was outside, Lynette said, "Sweetie, only in my dreams am I alone with a man as fine as him. Zane and I have been together so long, I feel like we've grown relationship barnacles."

"Oh, stop. You two are adorable." Like Jim and her, they'd met in high school and married right after graduating.

"He's so boring. And have you seen his beer belly? He looks fifteen months pregnant. Now, if I had a man like Coop…" She whistled. "What I could do alone with him in a closet for five minutes."

"Lynette!" Millie laughed, but couldn't help but be a bit jealous of her friend. Zane might've gained a few pounds, but at least he was alive.

"All I'm saying is that Jim's been gone awhile. If you and Coop gravitated together, well—"

"Stop right there."

"Valentine's Day is right around the corner. Mack Walker's planning a big shindig at his bar. My mom said he's trying to impress Wilma. There's even going to be champagne and a chocolate fountain. Doesn't get much fancier than that."

"I suppose not…" Would Cooper even go? If he did, what kind of woman would he take?

Speaking of the cowboy devil, he honked his truck's horn.

An hour earlier, the kids had gotten on the school bus. While she'd fed and bathed Clint, her brother-in-law had checked the horses and driven out for a quick look at the cattle.

"You know—" Lynette tapped her chin "—back in the day, wouldn't propriety have demanded Cooper not only watch over you, but marry you? Pretty sure it's even in the Bible."

"You're being ridiculous—not about the Bible—but your matchmaking." Millie shrugged on her red wool coat. "I don't even like Cooper."

"But even you have to admit he's as hot as July sun?"

Or possibly hotter.

Cooper again honked the horn.

Millie gave her friend one last hug and kissed her cheek. "Thanks for watching Clint. Hopefully, we'll be back before the kids get home."

"Go ahead and ignore me," Lynette shouted behind her as she walked out the door. "Mark my words, despite your sourpuss expression, the two of you are going to have a great day together!"

"Buh-bye!" Millie gave her well-intentioned but delusional friend a backward wave.

TWENTY MINUTES INTO the supply trip to Denver, Cooper had had just about all he could take of Millie's silent treatment. He got it. She wasn't buying what he was selling—only to his way of thinking, he wasn't offering her anything other than hard work and friendship.

"Warm enough?" He nudged the heat higher. Though the cold was still brutal, the wind had died and the sun shone.

"Sure."

"I felt bad for J.J. Poor little guy. Nothing worse than not getting a snow day you're expecting."

"Uh-huh." She stared out the passenger window as if the view was as riveting as a UFO landing.

"LeeAnn, on the other hand, looked happy about getting to school."

Millie sighed.

Cooper didn't care. They'd once been close. He might not deserve her forgiveness, but for some unfathomable reason, he craved it. And so if his chitchat already had him in hot water, he figured what did he have to lose by jumping right into a roiling-hot sulphur spring? "I've got a confession to make."

"Oh?"

"Or maybe not? You might already know." He glanced her way to find her gaze now tightly focused on the straight, lonely road ahead. The high plains landscape was gorgeous in its simplicity. The snow-peaked front range rose in front of them like a majestic dream. "Jim said he wouldn't tell you, but you two were probably close enough that he told you everything, huh?"

"Oh, for pity's sake…"

"What?" He hazarded another glance in her direction, only to lock head-on with her sparkling sky-blue gaze.

"Spit it out already."

"Okay…" He forced a deep breath. "Remember when Jim went hunting for a week in Wyoming?"

"What about it? He went hunting all the time."

"Yeah, well, that week he wasn't hunting, but with me."

"In Wyoming?" Her eyes widened.

"Norfolk. He crashed at my apartment. Seeing him again…" Cooper's throat knotted. Seeing his brother again had been surreal. And bittersweet. Jim had left with essentially nothing having been fixed. His little brother had told him to man up and make the first move toward repairing his relationship with his father. Cooper promised he would—soon. Just not soon enough, as Jim died two months later. If he had gone back then, would he have prevented both his dad's stroke and Jim's death? "Seeing him again was nice."

"Nice?" Millie's voice had taken on a shrill tone. "How very Cooper of you to drop a bomb like this then leave it sitting between us undetonated. You're such an ass."

"I'm not trying to be. I thought you'd want to know."

"That my husband lied to me? Apparently didn't trust me enough to tell me he was going to see his brother? Why would he lie about something like that when he knew no one pushed for a reconciliation for all of you harder than me? *Argh!*" She slammed the side window with the heel of her fist.

"Look, the last thing I wanted was to get you all riled up." The silent tears streaming down her cheeks made him feel all the more helpless, so he focused on the road and driving—apparently the only thing he could do without royally screwing it up. "I thought knowing might somehow help."

"Shut up, Cooper. I wish you'd never come home."
Me, too....

MILLIE'S FURY WAS the only thing keeping her upright during the endless day of errands needing to be run. Story of her life. Putting out fires with never enough water—meaning, cash.

In this case, she and Cooper were at Lowe's, standing side by side while looking at ready-to-assemble shed kits that could be used to replace the chicken coop.

"These are so far out my budget," Millie mumbled, shrugging deeper into her coat to ward off the wind's bite. "I might as well be buying a chicken Taj Mahal."

"Then let me take care of it," Cooper offered. "And since I'm not up on my Indian architecture, would you settle for a nice Victorian?"

Teeth chattering, she shot him a sideways glare.

He tossed her his keys. "See that Red Lobster?"

Maybe a couple hundred yards away in the next parking lot over sat the restaurant Millie hadn't before noticed. "Yeah. What about it?"

"Grab us a table. I'll make arrangements to get what we need delivered and meet you there."

"Don't be ridiculous. Do you know how much lunch out would cost? If you're hungry, I've got granola bars in my purse."

His jaw hardened—which should've made her dislike him all the more for growing impatient with her. But that steely determination he'd wielded at the farm supply store and now here, only made him more disgustingly attractive. Did he have any idea how much she hated conceding even that one point to him? That even with his whisker-stubbled cheeks ruddy from wind, he was still one of the finest-looking men she'd ever known? "You do realize that every second you keep us out here arguing is only making us both colder?"

Lord, how she hated to admit it, but he had a point. And it'd literally been years since she'd had buttery seafood. What the heck? If he was buying... After the bombshell he'd dropped on her that morning, the very least he owed her was a free meal.

"Fine," she said from between gritted teeth—they were chattering from the cold. "Want me to get you anything to drink?"

"Spiked coffee."

Twenty-five minutes later, Millie sat in a toasty booth, sipping from her own sinfully rich Bailey's and coffee. If only for a moment, she closed her eyes and slowly exhaled.

Everything would be okay.

She wasn't sure how, but she'd come too far to give up now. She and the kids and Clint had survived—even if not thrived, exactly—on their own, and despite Cooper's presence, she'd continue the tradition. She was a strong, capable woman and—

From the restaurant's entry, she watched Cooper approach.

Her mouth went dry and her pulse raced.

For a man to look so good ought to be criminal. Beneath his battered cowboy hat, even with his lips pressed into a thin, cranky line, he looked just as good back when she'd worshipped him in their high school cafeteria as he did now.

"Damn..." He eased into the booth and took off his hat to set beside him. "I'll bet the temp dropped twenty degrees just in the time it took me to walk across the parking lot. This mine?" He eyed his still-steaming mug.

She nodded.

He took a sip and groaned. The way he'd arched his head back and closed his eyes left her squirming. Did he have to make plain old coffee-drinking look obscene?

The waitress came and went, and while Cooper ate his weight in Cheddar Bay Biscuits, Millie picked at her Caesar salad.

"Something wrong with your food?"

"Not at all." Unless she paid attention to how much female consideration her brother-in-law unwittingly garnished. While he focused on food, at least a dozen hungry-eyed ladies apparently craved him! A fact that shouldn't have even bothered her, but did. Chalk it up to just one more reason why the sooner Cooper returned to his self-imposed exile, the better off they'd all be.

After a fortifying sip of her coffee, she picked up where they'd last left off on their meaningful conversation. "Did Jim tell you why?"

Cooper paused midbite. "You mean why he didn't tell you about his trip?"

She nodded while curling her finger around her mug's handle.

"Simple answer?" He dropped his biscuit on a saucer. "One that basically makes me feel like an even bigger pile of crap?"

Works for me...

"He said he would've rather spent the money on a trip for you and the kids, but—"

"I get it." And she did. How many times had she and Jim daydreamed about taking LeeAnn and J.J. to Disney? Yes, that money could've gone toward a once-in-a-lifetime trip—even better, been used to make house or barn repairs. But honestly? Now that she'd had a few hours to mull it over, her anger's edge had dulled. "I really do. And you know, as miffed as I am that he didn't trust me not to flip out at him over the money, it makes me feel…" Her eyes welled before she could complete her thought.

She glanced up to find Cooper's eyes shining.

He shocked her by reaching across the table to cover her hand. No—*shocked* would be too tame of a word. His tender, sweet touch *devastated* her. She wanted—needed—to hate him, but what was the point? The adult in her could rationalize that they were both the walking wounded. Granted, for different reasons, but Cooper had to be every bit as raw on the inside as she was. His guilt couldn't be any easier to bear than her grief.

They sat like that forever.

The restaurant's canned, easy-listening music and ambient conversations and clatter faded until all Millie heard was the thunder of her own heart.

It'd been three endless years since she'd been touched. *Really* touched. Sure, she hugged the kids and Peg and her friends, but that wasn't the same. This… This was indescribably good and maybe a little thrilling and made her long to just snuggle up against someone and release a long, slow exhale. Only when it came down to it, truthfully, she didn't want to be held by just anyone, but Cooper—the only guy she'd ever been attracted to besides her husband.

How twisted was that?

Wrong on every level, but she couldn't help how she felt.

She lifted her gaze only to collide with his. He looked

all at once apologetic and yet determined. But for what? Did he feel as flustered around her as she did him?

"Here you go." The waitress startled Millie back to reality—only, she didn't want to go. "An Admiral's Feast for you, sir. And, ma'am, your grilled shrimp skewer."

"Thanks," Cooper said.

"Need anything else?" the too-chipper, twentysomething blonde asked.

"We're good." Thank heavens her brother-in-law answered, because Millie didn't think she could.

Cooper withdrew his hand.

Losing not only his heat, but also his strength, felt akin to her bones having turned to jelly. No matter how deeply she'd resented his help that morning, deep down, she knew she needed him. He wasn't the enemy. Just another soul lost to what was beginning to feel like an almost insurmountable string of Hansen family tragedies. How would rejecting him, holding on to her frustration with him, make anything better?

They ate in silence.

Returned to the car with only polite chitchat.

She had to fix this, but wasn't sure how. "Thanks for lunch. It was delicious—but way too expensive."

"Stop."

"What?" She climbed into the truck beside him.

"Okay, it's like this…" A muscle ticking in his jaw, he stared at the busy street in front of where she'd parked. His profile was hard. Weary. Make no mistake, he was still one of the most handsome men she'd ever known, but his gaze used to hold an internal glow that'd gone out. Was any of the old Cooper left? Was she partly to blame for his now looking so downtrodden? "I'm a grown man. Don't tell me what to spend, or where to sleep, or how long I'm allowed to stay in the public areas of the house where I spent the first eighteen years of my life. For the hundredth time—sorry I hurt you. Sorry I never took the time to really get to know J.J. and Lee, but I'm trying… And if you'd just—"

Not thinking, just doing, Millie unfastened her seat belt and leaned across the truck's cab to kiss Cooper's cheek. But then he turned, and her lips grazed his. And her heart took off on a runaway canter fueled by sheer panic.

That kiss had been a total accident, so why were her lips tingling and a much lower heat pooling and her mouth turning dry and…

"Son of a biscuit, Mill, what was that?" Not only did Cooper cover his mouth, but as if she were a dangerously thorny cactus, he jerked a foot away.

Chapter Nine

Millie retreated to the relative safety of her side of the truck. "*That* was supposed to have been a platonic thanks-for-lunch kiss to your cheek, but you had to ruin it by turning."

"How have I ruined anything—I mean, at least, lately? Ever since showing up, I've worked my ass off and spent a bundle. You're the one putting on the big chill."

"I just kissed you!"

"That's my point—why the hell would you *ever* kiss me? You're my brother's wife. Kissing you doesn't—"

"Wait—you think I *for real* meant to kiss you? No, no, no..." She covered her face with her hands. "You totally misread the situation." But had he? Sure, she'd meant to kiss him on the cheek, only her body traitorously wasn't concerned about the mix-up. It'd been years since she'd kissed a man, and apparently, judging by her still-galloping pulse, she'd liked it!

What kind of horrible woman was she? Who kissed their brother-in-law? A straight-up harlot, that's who!

He started the truck.

"Don't you think we should talk more about this?"

Backed out of their parking space.

"It *really* was an accident."

Maneuvered the vehicle through the bustling lot.

"Cooper?"

Only after making a right onto the busy main traffic artery did he ask, "We still need to run by a grocery store?"

"No. Let's just get home." She crossed her arms. Fine. He wanted to keep up the silent treatment? Two could play that game.

A short while later, he pulled into the King Soopers in Thornton. Parked the car and killed the engine.

"I told you I wanted to go straight home."

His sideways half smile played teeter-totter with her heart. Not only did he bring back shadows of his brother, but more. He reminded her of the girl she'd been before taking her friendship with Jim to another level. Before then, she'd been Team Cooper all the way, worshipping him from the anonymity of crowded school hallways and rodeo stands. Her body seemed all tense and confused about the fact that she wasn't a lovesick teen anymore, and Cooper was no longer her crush.

After taking the key from the ignition, he said, "Only one problem with me taking you straight home."

She gulped. "What's that?"

"I got a hankering for something sweet last night, and, well…" His already wind-chapped cheeks further reddened. "I, ah, ate the rest of your private stash of Oreos."

The way he said *private stash* made it sound like her cookies were porn!

Now her cheeks superheated. "You're awful." And not just for eating her secret treats, but for making her feel all flustered and as if she'd lost control of her own body. Before he'd shown up, things like kissing and hugging and fornicating hadn't even been on her radar. Most days, she forgot she was even a woman. Now? Cooper had unwittingly made her crave something far more than cookies. And that fact shamed her to her core.

"UNCLE COOPER! LOOK what I made at school!"

Cooper looked up from his job of hanging heat lamps by chains from the barn's lower rafters to find J.J. charging his way, holding a shoe box under his arm.

It'd been two days since what he now called the *Denver Incident,* and his primary mission had become keeping a safe distance from his sister-in-law. Her cute son and daughter were another matter. Although LeeAnn wanted nothing to do with him, J.J. stuck to him like peanut butter on a cracker. The goofy kid was about as nutty, too. But in a good way.

"We've been learning about the ocean and stuff, and since my friend Cayden says Navy guys like you are swimming all the time, I thought you might miss the beach, so I made you this!" Out of breath from his long-winded speech, the kid finally stopped talking to grin. Lord, he was a cutie. Looked just like the pics of his dad at that age.

Cooper climbed down from the ladder to check out J.J.'s creation. For once, the weather wasn't half-bad. Temps in the fifties with no wind. "All right, buddy—" he ruffled the boy's hair "—show me what you've got."

J.J. lifted the box's lid to reveal a crude diorama of a beach scene. Though the sand contained scraps of paper and yarn, the water was made of blue construction paper, and a reef was constructed with painted rocks, Cooper's throat knotted upon seeing a green plastic army guy on top of the water. What he assumed was a scuba suit had been drawn on with a marker. "Is that me?"

"Uh-huh," his nephew said, "and that gray blob is a shark you were gonna save me from, but one of the coral rocks smashed it on the bus. Do you still like it?"

"Buddy, it's the most amazing thing I've ever seen. Thank you." With reverence, Cooper set the box on a ladder rung to give the boy a hug. "I love it."

"I love you, Uncle Cooper. I'm glad you live with us."

The words and resulting emotion struck Cooper like a punch. How could this kid *love* him? He hardly even knew him. But then maybe that was the magic of being a kid. They don't carry around a decade of regrets to use when judging a man's character.

To say Cooper was gobsmacked by J.J.'s affection was an understatement. He was also honored—and afraid. He didn't live with J.J. and his mom and sister and grandpa. As soon as Clint was back on his feet, Cooper was gone. What would his nephew think about him then?

"I, ah, love you, too, bud." What else could Cooper say? They were blood relations. Of course he loved him. But he also was unsure what that even meant. When Cooper returned to the Navy, as fast as J.J. had declared his affection, would he take it away?

J.J. squirmed from Cooper's hold and ran over to the calf's new enclosure. "Aw, you got his house made!" He opened the pen door and sat alongside the resting animal. J.J. hugged him. "You're so cute! I love you!"

Okay, wait… The calf was also getting J.J.'s love?

What did that mean in the grand scheme of things? Was the *L* word no big deal to kids? How was Cooper supposed to know? He'd talk to Millie about it, but after the kissing incident, he didn't trust himself to be anywhere near her.

Regardless of whether the kiss was accidental or not, it'd resulted in heat rocketing through him with the speed of a cracked whip. Not cool, considering who she was.

Their trek through the grocery store and the endless ride home had been torture. How did he begin to process the fact that by doing something as innocuous as turning his head, he'd changed everything? He'd always been aware of Millie. How sweet and kind and pretty she was. But now that kiss had added a shocking twist to her repertoire. It'd made him see her as not just his sister-in-law, or the friend she'd been back in school, but as a woman.

A desirable woman.

Even if his dad healed faster than anyone expected, it would still take a long time before he fully recovered. Cooper could potentially be stuck out here on the prairie for months. Not good.

Especially when he glanced toward his nephew still hugging the calf. That precious sight squeezed a long-forgotten place in his heart that was reserved for all things innocent and good.

In his line of work, he mostly saw darkness. The cumulative effects of which had fundamentally changed him. Left him doubting whether anything good was even left in this world. But looking at his nephew and the calf proved innocence was still possible.

But fleeting. Fragile. For the calf would grow and be sold. J.J. would grow and leave this lonely place. Cooper wouldn't be around long enough to witness either.

By THE TIME Cooper came inside for the night, supper had come and gone, and LeeAnn had taken over the kitchen table with her volcano construction. J.J. had finished his homework and was upstairs, playing his Xbox.

The harlot in Millie who'd enjoyed that kiss was glad Cooper had spent most of the past forty-eight hours in the barn. The nice person in her feared that in his attempt to steer clear of her, he'd work himself to death.

"Finished?" she asked while he hung his hat and coat on the back-door pegs.

"Yeah. The chickens and calf are toasty, and I'm sure the horses aren't minding the heat wave. I'll get to work on the new coop in the morning."

"Mill-eeee!"

"Duty calls." She looked toward Clint's room. "I made you a dinner plate. It's in the oven."

"Thanks. Smells good."

The whole time she helped Clint get ready for bed, she couldn't get her mind off his son. Did Cooper like her new pork chop recipe? Were he and LeeAnn sharing the table? After he ate, would he go to bed or share her TV time with her? Part of her wished he'd stay in his room. Another part wondered what it might be like for them to share a civilized adult conversation.

And more adult kisses?

Her cheeks blazed.

Clint tapped his whiteboard. It read *Where is he?*

"I assume in the kitchen, just now eating supper." The traveling nurse, a speech therapist and physical therapist had all visited. A change in Clint's meds had him less drowsy, more cantankerous and speaking a smidge more clearly. "He's always working."

Clint grunted.

"Don't believe me?" She outlined all that Cooper had recently done. And how now that her kitchen had been sanitized and spit-shined, she found herself missing the chickens and calf.

Clint wrote *Don't trust him!*

She sighed. "I don't mean to be disrespectful, but knock it off. He's done more around here in a few days than I could've in a month. You should be grateful to him. I know I am." Despite the tension between them that was as plain as summer heat on shimmering blacktop, not for a second would she discount Cooper's value to the ranch.

That kiss meant nothing. It'd been a split-second mistake to add to her ever-growing mountain.

Clint was back to tapping on his whiteboard. *He's the devil!*

"Oh, stop. You hating your son isn't going to bring your wife back. Do you think she'd approve of this feud? If anything, she'd be ashamed of you for not insisting Cooper come home years ago. Did you know Jim even secretly tried mending fences?" Whereas she'd initially been mad at Jim for lying to her, after letting the fact sink in, she now saw it as brave. When Clint was at full strength, he'd been a force to contend with. No one dared cross him.

Her father-in-law growled.

She gave him a dirty look. "Like it or not, Clint Hansen, things are changing around here for the better."

After giving him his meds, she made sure his lightweight plastic pitcher was filled with fresh water, and that his TV remote was on the nightstand in case he woke in the middle of the night. The physical therapist had mentioned that in the coming weeks, he wanted

Clint upright for a portion of his days. He also had simple exercises to do for regaining his strength.

"That should do it," she said after tidying his quilts.

"Thwank oooh."

She kissed his leathery cheek. "You're welcome. I love you. Now go to sleep and wake up less cantankerous."

In the kitchen, Millie expected to find Cooper at the table, but there was no sign of him.

"Where's your uncle?" she asked her daughter, trying to strike a casual, conversational tone as if his whereabouts didn't really matter. Which they didn't. She just wanted to know if he liked her pork chops. Because no way had she actually missed him the past couple of days.

LeeAnn shrugged. "Beats me. Do you think this is tall enough?"

After peeking in the oven to see if Cooper had even taken his plate—he had—she told her daughter, "Looks good to me. Maybe even it out on the back side?"

She sighed. "That's gonna take forever. God, this is so boring!"

"Sorry. Maybe you should've picked another project." Millie wanted to find Cooper, but instead joined her daughter in slapping more of the goopy papier-mâché strips onto her volcano.

What was it about him that had her craving his company? And why had she made that ridiculous speech about his staying away? If she hadn't, he might be in the kitchen, helping with this admitted snooze fest of a project. Was she a bad mom for hating the annual science fair? "How much do you have left to do after you paint your mountain?"

"Not much. The pop bottle eruption part seems super easy. Then I have to write the paper. And make the backboard. Oh—and find pictures for the backboard. Think Uncle Cooper would let me use a couple of his from Pompeii?"

"Probably. Does that mean you two are now friends?"

LeeAnn made a preteen look of disgust. "Eew, no. But his pictures were pretty cool."

"True…" Millie couldn't wrap her mind around how far away Pompeii actually was. She'd barely been out of the state. Would Cooper mind talking about his travels? What other pictures did he have? Was he one of those Navy guys with a woman in every port? If so, were they like girlfriends to him or just lovers?

Her cheeks flamed.

"Mom, are you okay?" LeeAnn froze with her hands in the glue and water mixture.

"Sure. Why?"

"You don't look so hot. Or I mean you do look hot—but all red and blotchy."

Thanks. *Just what every woman wants to hear…*

Millie helped LeeAnn finish, then they carried the volcano to the porch, setting it on top of the washing machine to dry.

"Mom, could I *please* use your cell to call Kara?"

Millie sighed. "Hon, we've been over this before. What's wrong with the house phone?"

"She's having boy problems and I need privacy. The house phone gets staticky in my room."

"Tell you what—" she kissed LeeAnn's forehead "—since I'm headed upstairs for a nice, long soak in the tub, that leaves the phone down here nice and private for you—although I'm worried about what you and Kara have going on that's so bad I can't hear about it."

"Mom..." Millie's child wielded preteen sarcasm like a burr under her saddle. It wasn't quite disrespectful enough to warrant punishment, but nonetheless annoying.

"All right, I'm leaving, but watch your sass."

Exhaustion clung to Millie's shoulders, weighing her down and making her movements sluggish. She lacked the energy to fish her cookies from out of hiding, and every stair felt like a mountain.

Cooper's bedroom door was thankfully closed.

Gunfire erupted from J.J.'s lair, meaning he was still playing one of those too-violent video games she hated. Jim had loved them all, and even as a toddler, J.J. enjoyed sitting on his dad's lap, helping shoot monsters. He had so few memories of his father, Millie didn't have the heart to take this one. She did at least limit his killing to dinosaurs and aliens.

"You about ready for bed?" she asked on her way into his room.

"Nope," J.J. said, "but Uncle Cooper is. He snores *really* loud."

Sure enough, big, strong Cooper had stretched out on a beanbag chair, using a pile of stuffed animals for a pillow.

Cheetah had stretched across his lap and actually purred!

In sleep, Cooper's expression looked softer. The concentration line between his brows all but vanished save for a thin line. His long lashes swept his whisker-stubbled cheeks. He truly was far too handsome for his own good.

Back in school, the girls who hadn't yet had their turn with him, loved him. The girls who'd loved and lost hated him. Since she'd been with Jim, that had landed Millie in the neutral zone in regard to feeling anything about Cooper. Now, with Jim's memory so distant, she'd forgotten his smell or even what it'd felt like waking up to him holding her. Where did that currently leave her status with Cooper? How many lovers had he left hating him all over the globe?

On the floor beside him was an empty plate. Did this mean he had liked her pork chops?

She put her hands to her yet-again flaming cheeks.

What was wrong with her? Why was her mind constantly in the gutter? Regardless of whether Cooper had eaten her chops or suddenly declared her the most fascinating woman in the world, the fact remained that he was her brother-in-law. Period. End of discussion.

"How about you turn off your game, brush your teeth and let me tuck you in."

"Mo-om..."

"Wrong answer. How about *yes, ma'am?*"

"Yes, ma'am. Just let me save."

Cooper stirred. "Sorry...didn't mean to drift off on you, bud. Did you get through Raptor Valley?"

Cheetah hopped down, only to vanish beneath J.J.'s bed.

All Millie could think was, *How come I don't look that hot when first waking?*

"Not yet, and Mom won't let me stay up."

Laughing, Cooper said, "When I was your age, I never wanted to sleep. Now that's all I want to do."

Fanning herself, Millie couldn't help but smile and nod. "True."

"Yeah, but you two are *really* old." J.J. turned off his game.

"I forgot." On his feet, Cooper stretched, which made him seem even larger beside her. He stood six-two. She knew, because Jim had been six foot even and complained about his big brother being taller.

"Your dinner was tasty." Cooper knelt to pick up his plate.

"Thanks." With her mouth curiously dry, Millie licked her lips. "Glad you liked it. The recipe was new." What in the world had possessed her to tag on that last bit?

"I liked the fennel."

What was she supposed to do with her hands? "You know about fennel?"

"In Pakistan, the locals roast it and chew it after dinner."

J.J.'s eyes widened. "You've been to Pakistan?"

"Sure have." Cooper fished his phone from his pocket and a moment later showed his nephew pictures of snow-capped mountains and an exotic-looking white building. "The temple is in Karachi. My friends and I were there looking for a bad guy."

"*Whoa*... That's cool! Did you find him?" J.J. asked.

"Sure did."

"Did you shoot him?"

"J.J.!" Millie gripped her son's shoulders, aiming him toward the bathroom. "Brush your teeth."

"Yes, ma'am..." If he pouted any harder, his bottom lip would touch the back porch stairs.

"Sorry about that," Millie said with her son out of earshot. "He's the product of too many video games."

"It's all right." With his phone back in his pocket,

Cooper's usual unreadable expression had slipped back into place. "He's a good kid."

"Thanks." Curiosity ate away at her—not to mention the fact that she craved hearing more of his story. Was there anywhere he hadn't been? Was he mostly working when he traveled, or did he often get a chance to do tourist things like he had in Pompeii? "Well? What did you do with the bad guy?"

The faint smile he cast in her direction ignited fireflies in her stomach.

"If I told you, I'd have to kill you."

Now her eyes widened. "It's *that* bad?"

He laughed. "I'm kidding. Honestly, I'm not sure what happened. After my team and I caught him, CIA spooks took over from there."

"Sounds dangerous." Millie nibbled her lower lip. While his stories fascinated her, she didn't like thinking of him in peril. Which was why she next blurted, "How many times have you been shot at?"

Wincing, he said, "More than I'd like to remember."

"Which means? Five? Ten? A hundred?"

He sat on the edge of J.J.'s bed. "For the most part, SEALs like to be phantoms—in and out of a place before anyone even knows we've been there. Every so often, plans go to shit—pardon my French—and then all hell breaks loose. Couldn't give you any hard facts on how often it happens. It's just part of the job."

"Getting shot at doesn't bother you?"

He shrugged. "Haven't much thought about it."

"But you could die…" And all of a sudden, that knowledge trampled the lightning bugs dancing in her tummy.

"Don't take this personally, but honestly? Since losing Mom, and then Jim—" he bowed his head, gripping the plate hard enough for his knuckles to whiten "—I haven't had all that much reason to live."

Chapter Ten

Cooper normally wasn't so chatty, and he sure as hell didn't know what'd possessed him to start up now.

"I—I'm sorry you feel that way."

"Is what it is," he said in his most matter-of-fact tone.

J.J. bounded into the room, dive-bombing the bed so hard that Cooper damn near lost his balance.

"Slow down, mister. I'm guessing your mom would rather tuck you in the bed, than scrape you off the wall."

The kid thought about that for a second, then busted out laughing. "Eeeew, gross! My pillow would be all full of guts and stuff!"

"J.J.!" Millie scolded. "Settle down and get under the covers."

What was up with that? Her always being so uptight with her kids? Had his mom been that way? Or had it been so long since her death that he couldn't remember standard operating procedure when it came to parenting?

When Millie approached her son, Cooper's senses went haywire. Only because he'd been so long without a woman, he found every inch of her attractive, from the way she smelled like the daffodils he used to pick out on the old Walker homestead to the faint rasp in her voice.

His nephew had scrambled under the covers. Minty-smelling toothpaste clung to the corners of his grin. "Can Uncle Cooper read me a story and tuck me in?"

"Honey, let's not bother him. He's—"

"I'd love to, bud. What do you want me to read?" While J.J. practically bounced from the bed to the bookshelf, Cooper tried deciphering Millie's dour look and failed. They used to be friends, but now he wasn't sure where they stood. He knew she didn't want him getting close to her kids, but even he could tell his nephew was desperate for a father figure. Jim had been gone a while. Had she ever thought of remarrying?

The thought of her hooking up with some random guy down at Mack's bar didn't sit so well.

"You about done?" Cooper asked.

"How about this one?" The human ball of energy was back in bed, tugging the quilts to his chin. "It's my favorite!"

"Captain Underpants?"

"It's really awesome," J.J. assured him.

Cooper looked to Millie for her endorsement.

She nodded. "It's a little out there, but all in good fun."

"Well, in that case…" Cooper couldn't resist giving J.J. a few tickles to his ribs, which sent the kid into a fit of giggles. "Let's start reading. This place could use some fun."

FUN.

An hour later, soaking up to her neck in the tub's steaming water, Millie tried focusing on what'd been the sweet sound of her son's laughter, as opposed to the man causing J.J.'s smile. Cooper had been spot-on about there having been no fun in the house for a good, long while, but what was she supposed to do about it?

Ever since Clint's stroke, there was so much work that even when Peg had been staying with them, Millie never felt caught up enough to indulge in lighthearted banter with her kids. Lately, it seemed like all she ever did was harp.

Brush your teeth. Do your homework and chores.

Far from being the fun, vibrant mom she'd always intended to be, most days she felt like an old biddy, constantly nagging.

How was it that Cooper hadn't even been in residence a week, and yet he was already the popular parent—and he wasn't even a parent, but an uncle!

It wasn't fair.

A knock on the bathroom door startled her. "Mill?"

She crossed her legs and covered her breasts with her hands. Her nipples instantly hardened. Damn, Cooper. "Wh-what?"

"Dad's hungry. What should I give him?"

A tranquilizer dart!

The moment the hateful thought struck, she tamped it out. What precious private time she found, she treasured, but she didn't have to take her annoyance at this intrusion out on poor Clint.

"Um… There's pudding in Tupperware tubs on the second shelf in the fridge."

"Thanks."

The hall floor was creaky, and she didn't hear him leaving. But then to be fair, she hadn't heard him approach. If he was still standing there, what was he doing? Was he as hot and bothered about her nakedness as she was? That pathetically thin door and a hundred-year-old skeleton-key lock were the only things keeping them apart. Well—those, and the fact that he was her brother-in-law, for heaven's sake!

"Mill?" he asked in a muffled tone.

"Y-yes?" Why had her breath hitched? Why did her breasts ache?

"Thanks again for dinner. You make a mean chop."

Before she could tell him he was welcome, the telltale creaky plank floor told her he'd already headed for the stairs.

Meanwhile, his praise for her cooking ignited a slow-burning fuse that led straight to an old-fashioned powder keg of irrational excitement.

What was wrong with her? Why did she feel like she'd gone back in time to their high school chemistry lab where, instead of focusing on her experiments, she'd studied the way the sun had perpetually tanned his neck? Back then, she and Jim had been friends, but not yet *more*.

Cooper didn't know it, but one of the biggest reasons she'd fallen for his brother was because of the time Jim had saved her from certain humiliation almost brought on by his big brother. She'd just worked up the courage to ask him to their school's annual Sadie Hawkin's dance when Jim strongly hinted that Cooper was hoping Bethany asked him. Sure enough, the two had not only gone together, but ended up dating for a couple months. If Millie had asked Cooper to the dance and he'd turned her down, she'd have been mortified. Millie had never forgotten Jim's act of kindness in giving her a head's-up regarding his brother's affections, even though years later, he'd admitted his reasoning hadn't been entirely altruistic since he'd wanted her to ask him to the dance! She had, and that first date had blossomed into a warm fulfillment that'd made her bone-deep content for all the years of their marriage.

Yeah? So what's got you so discontented now?

Millie scowled.

How come every time she saw Cooper, her mind dove straight to the gutter? Like back to that kiss.

Eyes closed, she couldn't help wondering what it would be like if he'd kissed her intentionally instead of just by accident? And then what if that accidental kissing had led to his becoming all rough and ready, dragging her across his truck seat to straddle him? And what if she'd been wearing a tank top, cowboy boots and her favorite long prairie skirt that just happened to hitch up? Exposing her bare thighs? And if she'd had on her good white-lace panties and her soft inner thighs rubbed against Cooper's rough, sun-faded jeans? He'd press his fingers into the back of her head, pulling her to him for a kiss that left her dizzy-punch-drunk and gasping. And then he'd rake his lips lower, down her throat and collarbone, all the while grazing his hands lower, too, until they weren't just on her lower back, but easing under her panties where her butt met the backs of her thighs.

He'd give her a teasing squeeze, and the erotic jolt might damn near make her faint. *"Darlin', you trying to do me in?"*

She'd giggle—no, deliver a sultry vixen laugh. *"Yessir. Is my scandalous plan workin'?"*

He'd groan, slipping those roving fingers of his—

Eyes wide open, splashing upright, Millie was mortified to find that she'd slid her fingers perilously close to giving herself a happy ending!

First thing in the morning, she'd start seeing about hiring an extra hand—just until Clint was back on his feet. Because for her own sanity, Cooper needed to go.

"I D-DON'T WANT it fr-from y-you!"

Cooper forced a deep breath. "Seeing how Saint Millie's upstairs in the tub, I'm your only choice in nurses. Now, you going to be a cantankerous old mule, or hush up and eat the damned pudding?"

Clint growled.

"I feel the same, Dad, but—" Tears stung Cooper's eyes. Frustration balled inside him, manifesting in him smacking the heel of his hand against the door frame.

His old man reared back in shock or maybe just surprise. Regardless, in that moment, he looked so frail that shame cloaked Cooper in sadness. How much time had been lost on this grudge?

"I h-h-hate you!"

"I know, Dad." Instead of moving away from his father, he moved closer. And then he pulled his too-thin frame into a hug.

At first, Clint fought him, but then the old man fell limp, and then with what little strength he had, he hugged back. Even immediately after his mom's death, Cooper had never heard his father cry, but he did now. The sobs were ugly and heartbreaking, yet strangely cleansing.

The harder Clint cried, the closer Cooper held him. And remembered the good times. And was so very grateful they weren't too late to start over.

"I'm sorry," he said.

His father issued his own garbled apology, and even though anyone else listening might not have understood,

Cooper did. The sentiment meant the world to him, as he'd been waiting a decade for not only his father's forgiveness, but also to come home.

Only Millie had made it clear this was no longer his home, but hers.

"DID YOU FIND the pudding?" Millie stood outside the still-steamy bathroom, holding a towel sarong-style around her breasts. She thought Cooper had still been downstairs, which was why she'd thought it safe to make a dash for her bedroom. Wrong.

"Sure did." His eyes were red. And teary. Had he been crying?

In the moment, his strangely sad expression trumped her awkwardness over her state of undress. "Everything okay?"

Though he nodded, she couldn't have said she believed him.

"Clint let you feed him without any complaining?"

His lips curved into a ghostly smile. "I wouldn't go that far, but yeah… He got the whole cup down."

"Great…" She shivered. Water droplets evaporated between her shoulder blades, but that didn't cool the heat pooling low in her belly. One look at Cooper's lips brought her all-too-rich fantasy of the two of them roaring to life. If she hadn't needed her hands to hold up her towel, she'd have clasped her flaming cheeks. "I should probably get dressed."

"Sure." He stepped aside, but she tried anticipating his direction and failed.

"Sorry," she said when they collided, wishing her every nerve didn't tingle with an exhilarating rush. Was she losing her mind? This was Cooper of all people. "I'm just gonna…"

They sidestepped each other two more times before she'd almost managed to reach the safety of her room.

"Hey," he said before she had the chance to step all the way in and close the door. "Mind if we talk a sec— that is, once you…" He gestured toward her electrified body, which only reminded her of her fantasy and how good his rough fingers had felt gliding along her—

No. Talking to him, looking at him, thinking about him was totally out of the question. "Sorry, but I'm really tired. In the morning—we'll talk then. Okay?"

He looked crestfallen. "Sure."

What did he even want to talk about? Cattle? J.J.? His father? What if it'd been something important?

"Good night."

"'Night." Her mouth went dry. Was he feeling odd, too? This curious sense of confusion whenever they shared the same space? "Cooper?"

"Yeah?" He'd turned away but now looked back. When their gazes locked, the air thickened, making it hard to think or breathe.

"Was it anything important?"

He shook his head. "Nothing that can't wait."

"Okay, well…" Why wouldn't her legs move? She wanted to stay here on her room's threshold with him, but also didn't. Her traitorous imagination just kept replaying him leaning in for a kiss. "Good night."

His eyes narrowed. "We've already been through that."

"Right." Beyond flustered, she bolted all the way into her room, shut the door and threw herself across the foot of her bed. What was wrong with her? She was a mom. A caregiver. A widow.

She was far too sensible for crushes, and even if she did have one, Cooper was the last man on earth she'd be attracted to—well, scratch that. Any woman in her right mind would be *attracted* to him, but that was different. She wasn't talking about something as shallow as finding him *hot*.

Then what are you talking about? her conscience nudged.

Even more to the point, what was she fantasizing about? Because her vision of him—*them*—had crossed every sane person's acceptable behavior boundary.

COME FIRST LIGHT, Cooper downed black coffee and instant oatmeal, checked on his dad to find him lightly snoring then fixed a bottle for the calf before shrugging on his brother's coat and heading out to the barn.

"Hey, fella..." he said to the little guy who stood in his pen, excited to see him—as opposed to the wide-eyed, startled-doe look he typically got from Millie. "Hungry?"

Cooper removed his gloves, resting them on the lip of a feed bucket. He liked the feel of the calf's warm, breathy snorts against his palm. He'd forgotten the simple pleasures of being in the barn when the sun rises. The way dust motes swirled in the sunbeams piercing through holes in the wood-plank walls. The rich scents of hay and leather. The sound of a light breeze whistling high in the rafters.

He took a deep breath, slowly exhaling.

"Had a big night," he said to his bovine pal. "Not sure how, but Dad and I turned a corner." He'd wanted so badly to share the miracle with Millie, but as usual, she'd treated him like a pariah.

What was she doing now?

Still snoozing until time to wake her kiddos? Or standing at the kitchen counter, looking sleepy-pretty in her fluffy pink robe? Lord, she'd grown into a fine-looking woman.

"Wanna hear a confession?" he asked the greedily suckling calf. "Yeah? Okay, well, true story—I'm a sucker for a woman in the morning." Messy hair and smudged mascara only heightened his pleasure. "I've always been a little jealous of my married friends." They were the lucky ones, waking up alongside their beauties every day—at least when they weren't out on missions.

Cooper sighed.

He could count on one hand the number of mornings he'd rolled over to be greeted by a welcoming smile. Sure, he'd been with his fair share of women, but precious few he'd cared enough about to spend the night.

Since his mother's death, Cooper had only lived half a life. On the job, he was all in and then some, but when it came to personal stuff, he was lost.

The barn door creaked open.

He glanced in that direction, expecting to see J.J. bounding in to feed the chickens. Instead, he saw Millie decked out in her pink robe and cowboy boots. Backlit by the sun, her tumble of hair formed a long halo. Her unaffected beauty quite literally took his breath away.

"There you are." Closing the door behind her, she hustled over to the calf, petting him, then warming her hands beneath his heat lamp. "Brr. It's chillier out here than I thought."

"Which raises the question—" he scooped feed for

the chickens, sprinkling it on the floor of their pen "—why are you out here?"

She used the toe of her boot to shift straw. "I felt bad."

"'Bout what?" He carried the chickens' water dish to the spigot.

"Last night. You wanted to talk, and I—"

"Forget about it." Because by the light of day, he no longer had the courage to open up to anyone—let alone Millie—about what had transpired with his father. Right after it happened, in the heat of the moment, he couldn't wait to share. But now he realized what a mistake opening up to Millie would be.

He already had a tough enough time physically staying away from her. If he ever let her emotionally inside? He'd be a goner.

Chapter Eleven

"Mom, eew!" Acting as if it were filled with worms, LeeAnn tossed her lunch sack to the counter. "You put J.J.'s gross bologna sandwich in my bag instead of my peanut butter."

"Sorry," Millie said in a not exactly sympathetic tone. *What was Cooper's problem?* She'd gone to the barn carrying an olive branch and come back with her arm a bloody stump. "Ever think you might be old enough to fix your own lunch?"

"I would," her daughter sassed, "but you always say I dawdle."

"You do." Millie switched the sandwiches, and even though she knew her daughter should be doing more around the house, she instantly regretted her sharp words. The kids had been through so much. What could it hurt for her to coddle them a little while longer? Besides, it wasn't LeeAnn she was upset with, but her uncle.

She felt like a darned fool. What had possessed her to traipse out to the barn like that?

"Mom?" J.J. wore his Transformers T-shirt inside out, and he hadn't even tried brushing his hair. "Have you seen my sneakers?"

"No, sweetie, but let's find 'em soon. The bus will be here any minute."

Ten minutes later, Millie had successfully gotten both kids on the bus, and now sat on the sofa holding an Oreo in each hand.

With a morning like this, what did that forecast about the rest of her day?

As if on cue, Clint hollered for her attention.

"Hold your horses," she hollered right back.

She'd already made most of his breakfast—just needed to add butter and sugar to his oatmeal.

She leisurely finished her cookies then trudged back to the kitchen to fix Clint's plate.

While she bustled around, Cheetah gave himself a bath on top of the fridge. She stuck out her tongue at the traitorous fur ball.

"Here you go," she said to Clint a short while later in his room.

Her smile felt forced. Most mornings, she enjoyed seeing the kids off to school and caring for Clint, but on this day, she'd have rather taken her entire bag of cookies upstairs to hide with under the covers.

Her father-in-law tapped his marker board. It read: *Where's my son?*

His son? This was a new development. Since when did Clint claim Cooper? "Last I saw him, he was in the barn." She stirred the melting pat of butter into the oatmeal. "By now, he's probably out checking the cattle."

"T-take m-me."

"To look after the cattle? We'll have to ask Peg about that. She'll be here tomorrow for the weekend."

He nodded, then pointed to his bowl, motioning that he'd like to take the spoon.

"You're not just eating your oats this morning, but feeling them."

He lurched for the spoon, managed to grab hold, but then spilled his first bite, which launched a tantrum.

"Simmer down." She wiped the mess from his pajama top with a warm, damp cloth. "This time, let me guide you, and we'll see if we can manage together."

He scowled.

"You don't like that idea?"

"D-do my-myself."

"I know you can, and I love that you're wanting to try, but—" He grabbed hold of her latest spoonful and flung it.

"Dad!" Cooper barked. "Knock it off."

Feeling as if she'd walked in on a movie that had already started, Millie was beyond confused by the sight of Cooper calmly curling his father's fingers around the oversize spoon his physical therapist had provided, then helping him guide it to his mouth.

"There you go…" Cooper's voice was gentle and patient, and certainly not from the same man she usually saw at Clint's bedside. "That's it, slow and steady. We'll get you back to normal in no time."

Millie stood on the sidelines until Clint had finished his entire meal—toward the end, even feeding himself for a couple bites. The change in not just his physical abilities, but also his attitude, was profound. Something had to have happened between the last time she'd tucked him in and now.

Millie tried helping Clint with his usual bathing routine, but he wasn't having it, and wanted only Cooper to help.

That afternoon, by the time her father-in-law's

speech therapist arrived, Millie stood at the kitchen sink, washing lunch dishes—or at least trying to. What she mostly focused on was Cooper. He was out back, wielding a chain saw to clear the remains of fallen cottonwood branches.

Before he could start on the chicken coop, the debris had to be cleared. It was a big job. The kind of thing she might've helped Jim and Clint tackle. Part of her thought she should head outside to lend a hand, but tensions between them had been running so high, what if he didn't want her anywhere near him? Besides, he was clearly capable of handling even this large of a task on his own.

It was already one on the gorgeous sunny day, and the temperature had apparently grown warm enough to warrant Cooper removing his shirt.

While the running faucet overflowed the mixing bowl she'd set in the sink, she couldn't help but visually drink the man in. The breadth of his chest. The definition of his abs. The way his faded jeans hung low on his hips and how he'd half-assed tucked his pant legs into his cowboy boots.

In raising the saw, his biceps flexed.

What would it feel like for him to hold me?

The moment the thought struck, Millie banished it. Clearly, the next time Lynette nagged her about dating, she might need to at least entertain the possibility. She and her husband had shared a healthy physical relationship, and she missed that aspect of her life. The only thing driving these inappropriate thoughts were basic needs for closeness and companionship. Plain and simple. No great mysterious longings for specifically Cooper, but essentially any man.

He'd cut quite a pile of limbs and turned off the saw. The sudden peace was welcome, but not as much as when he bent to gather logs for the woodpile. In the process, he offered mesmerizing views of his strong back, narrow waist and mouthwatering derriere.

She licked her lips.

"Holy mother of all that's good in this world..." Clint's speech therapist, Stacie, nudged Millie aside to fill his water pitcher from the tap. "A man that good-looking ought to be criminal."

"He's not so special..." Millie managed to say, though her mouth had grown painfully dry. *Liar!*

The pretty twentysomething female therapist whistled. "If you say so. Is he single?"

"*Cooper?* I suppose."

"How long's he going to be in town?"

Millie started to speak, but bit her tongue. Wincing, she raised her hands to her mouth.

"You okay?"

Millie nodded. "I'm fine. Thanks. And for the record, I'm not sure when my brother-in-law's leaving. I suppose as soon as his dad's back on his feet."

The therapist smiled. "Hmm... That gives me at least a couple months to get something going. And Valentine's Day is almost here. Mack's dating Wilma Meadows, and he's asking everyone to spread the word about a big party he's throwing at the bar. Know if he goes for my type—Cooper, not Mack?" Petite? Blonde? Flawless hair, makeup and nails?

Probably. "Gosh, I wouldn't have a clue."

"NEED HELP?"

"Sure." Cooper set a trio of fresh logs on the woodpile against the side of the house. "At this point, all there is left to do is haul the rest of what I cut. Looks like the coop's foundation is intact, so building a new one shouldn't be a big deal."

"That's good." They soon set into a rhythm. "I once saw a fancy chicken coop in that *Oprah Magazine.* Looked like a tiny Victorian mansion."

"That a hint?" His sideways grin gave wing to the butterflies that'd taken up residence low in her belly.

"Not at all. Just making small talk to pass the time."

He nodded.

"While I've got you, that was some miracle you worked with your dad."

His shrug did little to satisfy her curiosity.

"Did something happen? You know, like a breakthrough between you two?"

He placed his latest load of wood on the pile, then stretched, cradling the small of his back. "Why do you care?"

"Excuse me?" Before she could set her logs, he took them from her, in the process brushing against her in that maddeningly innocent way he had of driving her beyond distraction without having really done anything at all.

"You heard me..." He left her to get more wood.

"Wait—" Dawning was slow to come, but when it did, she chased after him. "Is this about last night? When you asked me to talk?"

"Drop it, okay?"

"Don't be like that."

"Mill..."

Upon his arrival, the last thing she'd wanted was for them to constantly be at odds. So why were they?

Knowing guilt knotted her stomach. She innately knew the reason they never got along, and the responsibility rested solely on her conscience. She was prickly around him, because of her physical attraction. It made as little sense in her head as it did in her heart. Nonetheless, that was the truth, and she'd never been the type to shy from blame.

"Coop?"

"What?" His terse tone made her wince.

"Just guessing, but when I made that ground-rules speech, I think you may have taken it a smidge more literally than I'd intended."

"How else was I supposed to take it? You pretty much made it plain that I'm not wanted. That said, even a blind pig could see you might not want me, but you damn well need me."

She cringed. *If you only knew...*

"You're right," she said. "I can't tell you how much I appreciate what you've already done." *And from now on, I promise not to let my apparent physical cravings interfere with common courtesy.* "I'm sorry about my earlier attitude."

"I don't need an apology. As soon as Dad's back on his feet, your problem will be solved when I'm gone."

Her throat knotted. Because of her harsh words, he viewed himself as a problem? If she was dead honest with herself, she knew nothing could be further from the truth. "Don't be silly. I appreciate your help more than you'll ever know. In fact, you've already made a transformation with your dad. What if you and I did the same?"

She met and held his gaze, wishing things could be different between them. That they could turn back the clock and be back in school, cracking a joke in chemistry class. Instead, she felt—

"Millie?" Stacie flounced out of the house in all her cute, young, disgustingly perky glory. "I'm all done! Clint did great!" She crossed the yard, holding out his monitor. "Thought you might need this."

"Thanks." Millie grit her teeth in annoyance. Couldn't Miss Perky Pants have stayed inside a few minutes longer? Or, better yet, left out the front door?

Stacie cinched her black satchel strap higher on her shoulder then crossed the short distance to Cooper, holding out her hand. "You must be Clint's son. I'm Stacie, his speech therapist."

"Good to meet you." After sharing his name, Cooper pulled the patented cowboy move of shaking her hand while tipping his hat. Lord, he looked good. And it made Millie sick that she couldn't help but notice! "Thanks for all you've been doing with my dad."

"Oh, it's my pleasure. How long will you be in town?"

"Just long enough, I s'pose." Classic infuriating cowboy response—long enough to be polite, but not convey any actual information.

Stacie didn't seem the least bit put off. If anything, his shortness only spurred her on. "Well, in that case, guess that means you'll be here for the big Valentine's Day party down at Mack's?"

"I'll be here," he said, his gaze roving off toward the south pasture. "But I'm not the party type."

"Well, you'd be doing me a *huge* favor if you switched that up." Big grin. Bat, bat of her lashes. "My creep boyfriend cheated on me with Allison—she's a waitress over at Maude's in Greenbriar. Anyway, the two of them are now an item, and since they'll be there, I wanted to show off my own shiny new toy."

A muscle ticked in his jaw. "Sorry, ma'am, but I'm not really the *boy toy* type, either."

"Oh, come on." She gave him an elbow nudge. "Millie, help me out here. How about both of you come? Peg's supposed to be here that weekend, right? I'll bet she wouldn't mind staying with Clint and the kids."

"Stacie…" Millie sighed. "This sort of thing just isn't me."

Miss Perky Pants pouted. "It'll be fun. You'll know everyone there. And who knows? Maybe you'll even find a cowboy all your own."

That suggestion raised Millie's hackles. First, if she wanted a man, she could darn well find one without Stacie's assistance. And second—well, she was too darn mad to even think of a second reason, but she was sure it was there somewhere. "You know what? I think I will go. And Cooper, you should go with Stacie."

The look he shot her way was darker than a spring thunderhead. "I. Said. I. Don't. Party."

"I know for a fact you drink beer *and* save people, so look on the event as an altruistic way to both save poor Stacie and down a few longnecks."

"Yaaaay!" Stacie said with a giggly leap, entwining her arm with Cooper's. "It's a date. And since I live all the way out by the county line, I'll just be here around seven that Saturday night. That way, we can ride together." Wink, wink. "We're gonna have a ball."

"WHAT THE HELL did you do that for?" Cooper asked Millie the second his *date* drove off.

"Do what?" she asked, all innocent, as if she didn't know exactly what he was talking about.

"You know *what*. I'm not going to be here much longer, and even if I were, dating a teenager is hardly on my agenda."

Millie grabbed an armful of logs. "Stacie's at least old enough to have graduated college. Besides, her suggestion that I couldn't find my own man really ticked me off."

"When did she say that?"

Men. "She just did. If you didn't get her undertone, then you must have earwax."

"Regardless, why'd you have to drag me into it? And since when are you on the prowl?"

"On the prowl?" She pitched her logs to their growing pile with a little more force than was probably necessary. "Jim's been gone three very long years. If I want to enjoy a little male company, I fail to see what business it is of yours."

Why did he get the feeling Millie was speaking a foreign language? "I never said it was…my business. Just that I didn't know you were interested in seeing anyone." *Because if I had—*

What? Would he have thought about asking her out himself? No. No way. He'd already caused his family enough shame. Putting moves on his brother's wife wouldn't exactly spit-shine his tarnished reputation. But then there was that accidental kiss. And the way last night, in the dimly lit hall, he'd wanted to press his fingertips to the water droplets glistening like diamonds on her collarbone. Don't even get him started on the way his body reacted to imagining her damp towel dropping to the floor. "If you are—ready to date, then sure. You should. It's not like you need my permission."

"I know." Why did her lips drop the slightest bit at the corners? Almost as if she was disappointed by his declaration.

"All right, then."

"Okay." Why was she all of a sudden breathing heavy?

Why was he doing the same?

"If you can handle the rest of this—" she thumbed toward the back porch "—I need to do laundry then fix supper."

"Sure. Go ahead." *And when you're done doing that, how about explaining to me why the real reason I'm on edge is because if I asked any woman to be my Valentine, I'd want her to be you....*

Chapter Twelve

"I've been thinking…" Cooper said to Clint. It was a sunny Thursday afternoon, and for once, the temperature hovered in the low sixties and there wasn't a breath of wind. "How about the two of us ride out to the catfish pond?"

His dad grunted, which Cooper would take as an affirmative.

"You want to wear your pj's, or one of those swanky new sweatsuits Peg brought for you?"

"R-real c-clothes."

Cooper laughed. "If by real clothes, you mean a nice, worn-in pair of Wranglers, sorry, but Peg would have my hide."

"R-real!" his old man roared.

"Okay… Let me see what I can find."

Since Millie was busy with the laundry, Cooper took the stairs two at a time to reach his father's old room. Opening the door was like opening a tomb, then stepping back in time. Nothing had changed since he'd last been there, kissing his mom goodbye before running out the door on that fateful night.

She'd sat at her dressing table, brushing her long hair. Every night, she'd faithfully counted one hundred strokes, then braided it before going to bed. Thinking of her only made his heart ache, so Cooper did what he'd grown best at—compartmentalizing his pain. He next fished through his dad's dresser for a pair of jeans and a red, plaid flannel shirt. Next came socks and his work boots. He spotted his dad's worn black-leather Stetson hanging on the back of the door, so he grabbed that, too.

Arms laden with Clint's duds, he damn near ran into Millie as she dashed up the stairs with a load of folded towels.

"What're you doing?" she asked.

"Man stuff."

"That doesn't sound good."

He shrugged. "It's a nice day. I figured Dad could use some fresh air."

"Probably." Her expression was unreadable as she rose a step higher than him. In the process, she accidentally brushed the length of her body against his. The sensation jolted his system. He wanted her. He couldn't have her. End of story.

Had she felt it, too? She stood staring, her kissable mouth partially open, eyes wide, breathing halted.

He had to get away from her before he went and did something stupid like tossing the damned towels down the stairs then pushing her up against the wall and kissing her till she begged for more—or maybe that would be him doing the begging? Either way, it couldn't happen, so he mumbled a goodbye, then carried on with his mission.

Back in his dad's room, he found Clint struggling to sit up, but in the process was coming dangerously close to falling out of bed.

"Whoa… Slow it down." Cooper raced over to help.

"At the rate you're going, you're only going to get hurt, and then Peg's going to hurt me."

"H-help…" Clint had spotted the clothes Cooper had piled on the foot of the bed.

It took twenty minutes of tugging and wrangling to get his father dressed. The process was no doubt embarrassing for Clint and humbling for Cooper. All his life, he'd been not afraid of his dad, but intimidated—no, that wasn't even the right word. Maybe it'd been more a case of unquestioning respect. No matter what Clint did, Cooper had been in awe. Only with his mother's death, that'd changed. He'd no longer viewed his dad as someone to respect, but hate. Only hate was also a complicated thing, as it implied a degree of passion fueled by love.

Once his dad was fully clothed, Cooper lifted him into his wheelchair, rolled him out to the old work truck, again lifted him into the passenger seat then repeated the whole process to get him back in his chair and onto the catfish pond's dock.

Once the task was done, and Clint sat at the end of the dock, tipping his face back to catch the sun, a profound sense of gratitude swept over Cooper. He was so glad to be home, back on his family's land. Back with his father he'd always loved, but had lost. "Dad?"

Clint grunted.

"You do know how sorry I am about Mom, right? And everything that happened after?" He knelt alongside his father's chair, staring at the ripples a light breeze stirred on the water.

His father held out his good hand, and Cooper took it. Clint gave him a squeeze.

The simple motion conveyed so much without his father having to say a word.

"Boy, am I glad to see you." The Friday before Valentine's Day, Millie gave her sister-in-law an extra-fierce hug.

"Uh-oh, has Dad been grouchy?" Peg unwrapped her scarf to hang it on the wall peg in the front entry. The sun shone, but blustery wind stole any warmth.

"Clint's doing great." Millie swallowed a lump of guilt. She wouldn't be admitting to Peg that the real reason she was happy for the visit had more to do with Cooper than her father. Millie welcomed the role of human buffer Cooper's sister would play.

"Then what's the prob—" Peg's smile faded. "Don't tell me my brother's been causing you trouble?"

Not in the way you probably think. "Cooper's been, ah, a huge help. Can't I just miss you?"

"Aw…" Peg ambushed her with another hug. "I missed you, too. So where is Coop?"

"Probably out in the barn. We had a tiff over Saturday night, and he hasn't said two words since."

Peg hung her coat alongside her scarf. "What's going on Saturday night?"

"Valentine's Day?"

"Geez, I totally forgot." Peg headed toward her dad's room. "But what's that got to do with you and Cooper?"

Millie gave her the abridged version. "I don't even want to go, but Stacie made me so darned mad, I felt possessed."

"What do you care if she goes out with my brother?"

Cheeks blazing, Millie was grateful her sister-in-law couldn't hear her galloping heart. "I don't. I just—"

"Wait just a minute…" Peg stopped Millie just outside her father's closed door. "You don't have a thing for Cooper, do you?"

"Of course not!" If her sister-in-law guessed Millie's dirty secret, was there any way Cooper could know? "I loved Jim very much."

"Who said you didn't? But, hon…" Millie's heart ached when Peg cupped her hand to her forearm. Millie didn't deserve her kindness, but she craved it every bit as much as her Oreos. "…Jim's been gone a long time. You're allowed to—" she elbowed Millie's ribs, then winked "—*you know.*"

Oh, did Millie know! How many times had she imagined what being with Cooper might be like? Only Peg wasn't talking about that particular scenario.

"In fact, I think this is a great idea—you getting out. You might even have fun."

Outlook doubtful.

"THANKS, AUNT PEG! I love it!" Saturday morning, Lee-Ann leaped from her seat at the kitchen table to give her aunt a hug for the fuzzy pink sweater she'd given her.

"You're welcome. You're going to look even prettier than you already are."

"Oh, wow!" J.J. was next to crush his aunt in a hug for the Matchbox cars she'd given him. "You're like the best aunt *ever!*"

"Hope so—" Peg tweaked his nose "—especially since I'm your only aunt."

J.J. laughed.

Cooper felt strangely disconnected from the family scene. On a lark, he'd bought the kids gifts the last run he'd made to town. Walmart had had a big Valentine's display, and a sentimental streak tugged his heart-strings. How many birthdays and Christmases had he missed? Once he left, how many more would he miss again? What would it hurt to now spoil his niece and nephew on a minor holiday?

The cat brushed against his leg, so he knelt down to pet it. The little guy had started sleeping with him, which made Cooper at least feel somewhat wanted.

Millie made a special Valentine's breakfast of strawberry pancakes and chocolate cherry muffins.

"Why don't you come over and join the party?" Peg stood next to him at the kitchen counter.

"I will." He smiled, but his sister's pained gaze quickly made it fade.

"I've missed you so much." Her voice cracked. "Thank you for coming. I don't know what we—especially Millie—would've done without you."

"It's no big deal." How could he accept her gratitude when, if he were a real man, he'd have returned home years earlier? He'd have stood up to his old man and for however long it'd taken, worked to regain his trust, respect and love.

"Yes, it is. And now that you're here..." She wiped silent tears and sniffed before enfolding him in a hug that conveyed more than words ever could. "Well, I'm just glad."

"Me, too."

"Uncle Cooper?"

He looked down to see J.J. "What's up, bud?"

"Who're those presents for?" He pointed to the sack filled with crudely wrapped gifts that sat at Cooper's feet.

"What presents?" He grabbed the boy under his arms, swooping him high, loving his shrieking giggle.

The cat bolted off.

"You mean those?"

"Uh-huh," J.J. said when Cooper set him back on his feet.

Cooper lifted the sack onto the counter, drawing out two boxes of chocolate turtles. "These are for your mom and aunt." He presented them with a flourish.

"You shouldn't have," Peg said, already tearing open the plastic wrapping, "but I'm sure glad you did."

Millie held her box over her heart. Her eyes shone. Had her last Valentine come from his brother? "Thank you," she softly said. "These are my favorite."

I know. One long-ago night when they'd both been in middle school, they'd been at a fall carnival, playing bingo and eating pizza when she'd won. She'd had her pick of prizes. Gift certificates and video games and even lift tickets for Copper Mountain. What had she picked? Turtles. "I'm glad you like them."

She nodded, then looked away, ending the moment— if there'd ever even been one.

"Is there anything in that bag for me?" J.J. jumped while asking.

"Maybe," Cooper teased. "But ladies first. Here, LeeAnn…"

Never having been his biggest fan, she eyed the poorly wrapped box with suspicion but then cautiously tore the red, cupid-sprinkled paper. He held his breath when she removed the stuffed pink teddy bear that held a silver heart necklace and matching earrings, as well as a mini-iPod. Her smile was swift but then faded, almost as if she was forcing herself not to show emotion.

Cooper's heart ached. How long until she accepted him like her brother already had?

"Thank you," she said. "The bear's super cute and I love the jewelry and iPod."

"There's an iTunes card in there, too." Cooper wasn't sure what to do with his hands. He'd never been awkward around the fairer sex, but LeeAnn and her mother were a tough crowd. "Figured you'd need it to buy songs."

LeeAnn looked at him as if she wanted to say more, but didn't.

"Want me to help you put on your necklace?" Millie asked.

LeeAnn shook her head before putting all of Cooper's gifts back in the box. "I don't have time. Remember? Kara's mom's picking me up. We're going to an IMAX in Denver then for pizza and a sleepover. You already said I could like a week ago."

"I remember," Millie said. "Sorry. Just slipped my mind."

"Since she's having a sleepover," J.J. asked, vrooming one of his cars across the table, "can Cayden spend the night here?"

Millie opened her mouth, but Peg beat her to the punch. "Since I'm in charge tonight, how about Cayden comes *and* we have something extra special for dinner?"

"Like popcorn and candy bars?"

Peg laughed. "Sounds perfect."

Millie said, "How about at least adding a banana and glass of milk?"

J.J. pouted. "Okay…"

Though Cooper hardly felt part of the cozy holiday

scene, he wanted to be. After clearing his throat, he said to his nephew, "Bud, there's one more present in my bag. Bet it's for you."

"Yaaaay!" Hyped up on three sugary muffins and the couple of pieces of candy he'd already pilfered from his aunt, the kid hopped to accept Cooper's gift. "What is it?"

"Why don't you unwrap it and find out?" Millie suggested before glancing Cooper's way. Had he imagined it, or had her expression softened?

J.J. tore into his gift, then went haywire. "Oh, my gosh! It's a Wii! It's a Wii! I gotta call Cayden!"

"Slow down." Millie snagged his arm before he got to the phone. "Isn't there something you need to do first?"

"Brush my teeth?" He'd scrunched his freckled face in confusion.

"How about thank your uncle?"

"Oh, yeah! But he already knows I love him. I told him the other day." J.J. gave him a fast hug. "Thank you, Uncle Cooper! This is like the best present I ever got in my whole life! You're awesome!"

"You're welcome, bud. Glad you like it." He ruffled the kid's hair, trying to play it cool when he felt like bawling. LeeAnn and J.J. weren't just random kids, but his family. His blood. Every once in a while, when he looked at LeeAnn, she reminded him of his mom. And J.J. had all of the Hansen men's green eyes. Cooper had many great friends back in Virginia, but they weren't family. As much as he respected and admired them, their smiles had never tugged at his heart. "Go on," he said to J.J., "call your friend."

Honestly, Cooper needed the space. He wasn't sure

how to cope with all this touchy-feely stuff. He'd been trained to stifle his emotions. So how come now he felt like the walking emotionally wounded?

His natural instinct was to hide out in his room.

Instead, he went to sit with his father. Over the past few days, he'd been reading to him. Cooper's SEAL friend, Grady, had gotten him hooked on vintage sea stories, so he'd started Thor Heyerdahl's *Kon-Tiki*. "Feel like listening to me ramble?"

His dad scribbled on his whiteboard: *Do I have a choice?*

The words might've been harsh, but his old man's eyes were smiling. Cooper took that as a good sign.

He grabbed the book from on top of the dresser, opened it to page seventy-eight then settled into the corner armchair to start reading.

"I THINK WE have you to thank for this."

"What do you mean?" Cooper asked his sister after they'd shut the door to his father's room. Clint had eaten double his usual portion—mostly accomplished under his own steam—and Peg's awful jokes had even coaxed a few smiles. Once his night meds kicked in, though, he was out.

"Dad's improved more in the time you've been here than he did in all the weeks before you'd arrived."

Cooper shrugged. "I wouldn't put too much into it. He's got a lot of good people in and out of here all the time, helping him."

"Don't sell yourself short. Millie told me that at first, things between you and Dad were plenty tense, but then something changed. What happened?"

They'd moved into the entry hall and Peg sat on the third stair.

"Guess it's hard to pinpoint. One night, I think he came to the realization that I wasn't going anywhere, and meant him no harm. I apologized for Mom—at least, as best as I could." He bowed his head. "But we both know, no mere apology is ever going to make that right."

She rose to place a comforting hand on his arm. "Just so happens, I've had a few years to ponder the issue, and as simplistic as this might sound, I think that apology of yours wasn't even necessary. It was implied, you know? Of course you were sorry for what happened. We all were—are. But when it came down to it, Dad wanted you here to use as a verbal punching bag, and now he wants you back as his son—to try to put the pieces back together."

Cooper pulled away from her to peer out one of the front door sidelights. "But I'm not back. I'm not even capable of being the son he wants me to be."

"How do you know you're not already? Have you seen the scrapbook he keeps of you? The Navy sent announcements for every step of your journey. He might not have come right out and said it, but he's proud of you, Coop. So am I. Everything's gonna be all right. You'll see."

He happened to look up.

Millie stood at the top of the stairs. She wore a tight-bodiced, flare-skirted red dress with red cowboy boots. She'd left her hair down—long and wavy. Just the sort of style he'd like to run his hands through while kissing her thoroughly out behind the barn. She looked beautiful. The perfect Valentine jewel. Only the joke was on him, because she wasn't his—would never be his. Even if she wasn't his sister-in-law, she deserved the kind of sage, family man who'd stick around. Someone like Jim—a saint of the sort Cooper would never be.

His sister must've caught him ogling, as she followed his gaze. "Oh, Millie... You look gorgeous!"

"You think?" Millie asked with a twirl. "Are the boots too much?"

"It's Valentine's Day. Anything goes as long as it's red or pink."

"Oh—well, in that case, maybe I should add a feather boa?" Millie's laugh did funny things to Cooper's stomach. He didn't want Stacie to show up. He wanted to take Millie and her red dress and boots out for a nice steak dinner, then maybe go for a few slow turns with her around a dance floor. She peered down at him and frowned. "Cooper, you haven't even had a shower? Your date's going to be here in ten minutes."

"For the last time," Cooper said, "she's *not* my date."

Hands on her hips, she gave him a cocked-head sigh. "Whatever you're calling her, Stacie's arriving in ten minutes. We're meeting Lynette and Zane twenty minutes after that."

"Yes, sir, Master Chief." Mounting the steps, he saluted her on his way past, wishing she'd skipped the pretty floral perfume that made him crave doing more with her than dancing.

"COULD SHE BE any more obvious?" Millie wasn't normally the judgmental type, but the way Stacie had the audacity to squeeze Cooper's buns while they were two-stepping made her want to hurl.

"Who?" Lynette was too busy ferreting M&Ms out

of the snack mix in a bowl on the table to be bothered with looking up.

"Who do you think? Stacie's done nothing but grope Cooper ever since she showed up at the front door. And don't even get me started on her cleavage. J.J. had a friend over, and I felt like locking the two boys in J.J.'s room until *Boobs on Parade* left the house."

Lynette laughed hard enough to choke on her beer, which resulted in much coughing and a trek to the crowded restroom. By the time they got back to the table, Mack's new girlfriend, Wilma, had cleared the dance floor and given the homegrown country band a break.

Wilma wore a red gingham square-dancing dress, and her platinum hair was tall enough that Millie guessed she prescribed to the old adage: *the higher a woman wore her hair, the closer she was to the Lord.*

"How y'all doin'?" Wilma had hijacked Mack's party, and sashayed up the two steps leading to the stage as though she owned the place. She took the microphone. "Havin' fun?"

"Yeah!" the crowd cried in a chorus of raised beers and some hard stuff.

Millie clamped her lips shut.

Stacie had Cooper pinned alongside the jukebox and put on a show of laughing at every little thing he said. Personally, Millie had never found the man to be funny or a particularly scintillating conversationalist.

Liar...

Lynnette set down her third beer and said, "Stare any harder, and you'll set the poor girl on fire."

"What're you talking about?"

Zane returned with a metal bucket filled with more

brews. "There's quite a line at the bar. But never fear, ladies, your prince has returned. Drink up."

"Quit hamming and kiss me!" Lynette had had just enough to drink that she was apparently feeling frisky.

Millie still nursed her first longneck bottle. She wanted her wits about her to keep tabs on Stacie.

While Wilma rambled on about the upcoming couples-only dance, Millie glanced wistfully at her best friend, currently engaged in a sweet-spirited make-out session that made her jealous clear to her toes. Even in the center of the big crowd, loneliness consumed her. Since Jim's passing, who had she become? She was still a mom and a daughter-in-law, but no longer fully a woman—not in the way that mattered on this night dedicated to romance.

"Now that y'all know the rules," Wilma prattled on, "I want *only* couples out on this dance floor. Midway through the song, my fiancé…" The crowd took a minute to soak in the fact that Wilma wagged her diamond-clad ring finger for all to see.

A cheer broke out, then plenty of congratulations to Mack and his bride-to-be. At least the fact that she seemed to have assumed hostess duties of what was supposed to have been Mack's party now made sense.

Millie couldn't have felt lower than a mouse in a snake's belly. Making matters worse was Stacie, pushing Cooper onto the dance floor already crowded with couples. Apparently, he'd had just enough to drink to go along with her request.

"Thank you, thank you," Wilma gushed, "but let's get some other couples in the mood for love. Now, whoever Mack picks as most romantic couple on the dance floor is gonna win a free bucket of beer! Any questions?"

Chet Myers shouted from the bar, "Why can't us single guys win beer?"

Wilma dismissed Chet's comment. "Seriously, folks, we've got great games coming up for any singles who wanna find romance, but for now, this dance is for our couples. Remember, let's keep it clean, but most important, get romantic for Valentine's Day!"

The rowdy crowd erupted in a round of wolf whistles and cheers.

"Here we go…" Wilma signaled the band to start playing, and couples twirled round and round.

Stacie and Cooper stood close enough that a piece of straw wouldn't have fit between them.

Millie swigged her beer.

The two of them were disgusting. And cheaters! How did they technically qualify as a couple when this was their first date?

The crowd went wild when Mack hammed it up, gesturing for the crowd to choose which couples were their favorites.

Of course, Stacie and Cooper drew a big round of applause.

Millie's cheeks felt hot enough to be catsup-red.

Could Stacie be any more obvious? What the woman did with her hips was obscene!

The band started in with a nice and slow country love song.

Wilma shouted, "Think we have some lovers in this bunch?"

More drunken hollers raised the roof.

As much as Millie was tempted to run home to hide

under her covers, all it took to convince her to stay was one look at Stacie with her hands in Cooper's hair and him not looking like he minded. Well, she'd show him a thing or two about flirting!

She pasted on her brightest smile before grabbing Buck Evans by his right arm. They'd gone to school together, and he used to be married, but his wife left him to launch her Vegas dancing career. Word had it she was a stripper, but Buck referred to her as a show-girl. "Wanna dance?"

"Ah, sure. I guess."

"Great. Come on." She couldn't get out on that dance floor fast enough. Two could play this game.

"I'm not a very good dancer," Buck said.

"That's okay," she assured him.

"Looks like we have a late entry!" Wilma shouted from the bandstand. "What do you think, y'all? Do they make a good-looking couple?"

Cheers erupted.

After a few more minutes of twirling, the music stopped, and along with it, Millie's heart.

Cooper stood right next to her, looking so stupid-handsome she could cry. What was it about him that made it impossible for her to even think of any other men? She didn't want him, but she sure didn't want Stacie fawning all over him, either.

Mack joined his fiancée on stage.

"Mack, hon," Wilma said, "who do you think deserves our first free bucket of Valentine's Day beer?"

Above her pounding pulse, Millie heard expected wolf whistles and few off-color comments.

What she didn't expect was to feel physically ill when Mack pointed at Stacie and Cooper then said,

"Sorry to the rest of you folks, but those two look like they have what it takes to go the distance. Good luck to our happy couple!"

"Sorry we didn't win," Buck said. "If you want, I'll buy you a beer."

"That's okay." She delivered a warm pat to his arm. She shouldn't have used him like that. It was childish and beneath her. "You go on and have fun."

"You, too, Millie." He tipped his cowboy hat. Now, see? Why couldn't she be attracted to a nice, courteous guy like Buck? Why was her taboo brother-in-law the only man since Jim who'd made her heart beat faster?

While accepting their prize, along with a whole lot of smooching, the couple was gifted with cheap plastic crowns proclaiming them Romance King and Queen. When Stacie got a little too excited, dropping her crown onto her cleavage then staring expectantly at Cooper as if he should retrieve it, Millie felt like throwing up. Knowing she couldn't take too much more, she turned her back on the happy couple and aimed for the bar. Screw beer. She needed tequila!

She'd just downed her second shot when a familiar voice behind her said, "Thank God I found you. Please help."

Cooper had sidled alongside her—or he could've been a tequila-induced mirage. But she didn't think she'd had *that* much to drink.

"I need you to dance with me—you know, pretend we're an item so Stacie leaves me alone. You might even throw in a kiss for good measure—might look more convincing."

She wrinkled her nose. "Mr. Romance, why would

I want to dance with or kiss you when you've clearly found your soul mate?"

He scowled. "Cut the sarcasm. I was playing along with this whole damned thing just to be polite, but now that she's getting serious, I need an escape route, and pretending to be interested in you is my only logical path. Are you in?"

Gee, that had to be the most romantic proposition she'd ever had—*not!* Still, if it got Cooper away from Stacie, Millie was all for trying. While Millie didn't want to be with him romantically, she was certain Stacie was no good. Why, she couldn't say right at that moment. Regardless, as Cooper's sister-in-law, she'd be doing not just him, but her entire family, a favor in sheltering him from Stacie's wicked ways.

"Come on, Mill, give me an answer. She's headed this way."

Stacie fluffed her hair as she walked, then adjusted her push-up bra for maximum cleavage. She wore enough lip gloss that if she went in for a kiss, poor Cooper would see his reflection.

His expression turned desperate. "Screw the dance. You know what desperate times call for, and this is one of those occasions." He slipped his arms loose around Millie's hips.

"Wh-what're you doing?" she asked, wishing his touch didn't feel so darned good.

"Leaning in to kiss you. *Please,* just go with it."

Terror struck until Cooper's warm, yeasty breath melded with hers. At first, his kiss was soft, testing. But then he increased his pressure until lightning bugs took up residence clear from her chest to her toes.

When he stopped, he whispered, "Think it worked?"

Millie peeked around his shoulder to find Stacie with her hands on her hips, looking madder than a racked bull.

In the meantime, Millie's lips still tingled from Cooper's kiss—even more alarming was the fact that she craved more. The walls closed in around her. The smoky, too-warm air. All the people. The smells. Cologne and perfume. Beer and whiskey and cheeseburgers.

The band had started playing again, and Stacie was kicking up a fuss about Cooper, and how he was supposed to have been kissing her.

A low, tight knot formed at the back of Millie's throat, and she feared the only way to find release would be an ugly round of tears. Not only was she embarrassed, but ashamed, too. No matter what the reason, she'd had no business kissing her brother-in-law. Period.

Millie pushed through the crowd, running for the bar's rear exit.

She pushed open the door only to gulp in fresh night air. The cold came as a welcome relief to the suffocating warmth inside.

When her sobs hit, they weren't pretty, and she hid between the Dumpster and a couple of old trash barrels.

"Mill? You out here?"

Great. Her Valentine had stepped outside for a visit—no doubt to laugh at her just like everyone else in the crowd. The last person on earth she wanted to see was Cooper. He was smart enough that he should have known she'd want nothing to do with him.

"Go away," she snapped.

"There you are…" He'd carried his pea jacket and now slipped it over her shoulders.

She welcomed the warmth, but most of all, her body traitorously craved his masculine smell. The leather and musky citrus she'd grown to recognize as being uniquely his. "Thanks."

"You're welcome. Mind telling me what you're doing out here?"

"Isn't it obvious?"

"Not entirely…"

She sighed. "To spell it out, I'm mad at you for making a fool out of me in front of damn near the whole town. You never should've asked me to kiss you. And I never should've agreed. No matter how compelling your excuse may have been, I should've been strong enough to deny you. Most of all, I'm mad at myself for ever being goaded into leaving the house in the first pla—"

Before she could finish her rant, he cupped her face between his big, rough hands, silencing her with another kiss. This one slower and sweeter, transforming the cruel February night into a balmy summer in her heart. Only Cooper had no business being anywhere near her heart, which was why she pushed him away. "Stop."

"Sorry. Must've been the beer."

Just when she thought she couldn't have sunk lower, he'd had to go and blame kissing her not once, but twice, on being drunk?

Millie raised her hand to slap his damned handsome face, but he caught her wrist on the way up, leaned in to kiss her again then tossed her the truck keys. "Once you've sobered up, mind giving Stacie a lift back to the house? I'll find my own ride."

Chapter Thirteen

"He did what?" Peg whispered so as not to wake the boys, who'd made a fort in J.J.'s room. Half of it hung out in the hall, so they couldn't shut J.J.'s door. Cheetah seemed fascinated by it, and sat under the ragged sheet canopy. "Start over from the beginning."

She and Millie sat cross-legged on Millie's bed, holding the bag of Oreos between them. Millie told her about the dance contest, and how Cooper wanted her to serve as a dating decoy for Stacie, but left out the part about him kissing her again behind the bar. "You can't imagine how awkward it was when I had to tell Stacie he'd taken off—God only knows where. Plus, I had his coat. For all I know, he could be frozen in a ditch."

Peg snorted. "He's a Navy SEAL. Pretty sure he'd find a way to survive in Antarctica with tooth floss and a napkin."

"Still…" Millie sniffed. "It was a horrible night. Lynette's mad at me for leaving. Zane's mad at me because I got Lynette upset—the whole thing was a start-to-finish disaster."

"Okay, wait—go back to the part about the kiss." She took another cookie from the bag. "Out of morbid curiosity, how was it?"

Millie's eyes widened in panic. She couldn't very well say it'd been as sweet as downing a hundred bags of Oreos, so she forced a deep breath, crossed her fingers and lied. "The kiss? Um, it was okay."

"Just okay, huh? Show me your hands."

The heat in Millie's traitorous cheeks rose twenty degrees. "Why?"

"Because I have a feeling that behind your back, you're crossing your fingers. It's okay if you liked kissing him. I know you loved Jim, but sweetie, it's been a long time since he passed. He wouldn't want you to spend the rest of your life pining."

"True, but he also would never want me to forge a new life with his brother of all people—not that such an option is even on the table."

"I can see that…." Peg fussed with the cookie bag's Ziploc. "But this morning, when he gave Lee and J.J. their gifts, I saw the way you looked at him—the way J.J. looked at him. You feel something. J.J. clearly thinks Cooper hung the moon."

Millie interjected with, "LeeAnn can't stand him."

Peg laughed. "Lee can't stand anyone. Goes with the age."

"True." Millie couldn't help but laugh, too. But then her throat knotted. She had enjoyed Cooper's kiss. Too much. She could have kissed him all night and deep into the next morning, but at what cost? She was already financially broken. When Cooper left for Virginia, was she emotionally stable enough to suffer a second broken heart, as well? Of course, she didn't officially feel anything romantic toward him now, but as much as she'd already grown to crave his company, she had a sneaking suspicion that he'd be all too easy to love.

COOPER JOGGED THE first ten miles to the house then cut across the pasture once he'd reached family land. Anyone outside of his SEAL team would probably think him nuts, but the run felt good. He was used to driving his body hard, and he'd run greater distances, in far colder temps while soaking wet. As he was dressed in a T-shirt, chunky sweater, jeans and deck shoes, this trek was a cakewalk. Hell, he didn't even have his heavy-ass backpack to worry about.

Unfortunately, by the time he reached the barn—he wasn't yet ready to go in the house and face his sister or Millie—he realized that while he may not have physical worries, he did have a fair amount of explaining to do.

Truth was, all night long he'd secretly hoped to kiss Millie. He didn't give a shit that it'd been in front of practically everyone he'd ever known outside of the Navy. Maybe deep down he'd wanted it that way? Just to get everything out on the table in a one-stop, efficient manner. But had that been fair to her?

Moreover, what was the point in declaring his intentions toward her when he wouldn't even be sticking around?

He groaned.

Sassy released a soft snort.

"How's it going, girl?" When he rubbed the horse's nose, she leaned into his touch. "What I wouldn't give if all women were as uncomplicated as you."

The calf and chickens were down for the night, content beneath their respective heat lamps.

Now that the mess left by the fallen tree had been cleared, that meant he was good to go on assembling the new chicken coop. He hadn't mentioned it to Millie, but he'd remembered her saying how she'd once seen a fancy chicken coop and thought it was cool, so that was exactly what he planned to give her.

She deserved so much.

Only a fraction of which he was equipped to deliver.

Had the night gone the way she'd deserved, that kiss wouldn't have been an excuse for ditching Stacie, but so much more. As much as it pained him to admit, what she'd really deserved was a surprise kiss from a real man—maybe even that guy Buck, whom she'd danced with. She needed the sort of man who'd care for not only the ranch, but her and the kids, as well. He'd be a worthy son for Clint.

In short, Millie deserved a man who was everything Cooper wasn't.

"WHAT'RE YOU STILL doing up?"

"What's it look like?" Millie hadn't meant to be sharp with Cooper. Or maybe she had.

He closed the back door behind him.

She shivered from the burst of cold air.

"Let me rephrase my question." He drew out the chair across from her, spun it around then straddled it. He was tall enough to rest his forearms on the chair's back. His cheeks were ruddy from the cold and his grown-out hair adorably mussed. Couldn't he at least have the decency to look bad? "Why are you up at 1:00 a.m. painting LeeAnn's volcano?"

"The science fair is next Friday. She needed me to put a coat on for her this afternoon so it'd be dry enough tomorrow for her to start adding trees, but with all the party planning, my day got away from me."

"You outshone every woman in that bar."

"Hush." If her heart beat any faster, she'd pass out, doing a face-plant in the ugly brown paint.

"I mean it. I'm sorry I ran out on you, but I'm not sorry I kissed you."

"Cooper Hansen, I'm about two seconds from pitching this paint in your face. Do you have any idea how humiliated I was to not only go back into that bar alone, but having to explain to Stacie that you'd left her, too?"

"She get home okay?" He at least had the decency to bow his head.

"Well, gee, I wouldn't exactly know, seeing how about two seconds after I told her you'd left, she took off with some other guy and told me she'd find her own way back to her car."

He had the gall to grin, and he looked damned sexy doing it. "Guess since her car's not in the drive, my question was irrelevant."

"You think?"

"Ouch." He was back to grinning.

Millie wanted to slug him. Trouble was, she also wanted to kiss him. Instead, she fished one of the Oreos from her nearby Ziploc bag.

"I told you I didn't want to go out with her." He shrugged. "To my way of thinking, right from the start, that makes this whole mess your fault."

That's it—she put down her half-eaten cookie to dredge her paint brush across the paper plate then flick it at him. Unfortunately, more of the washable poster board paint landed on the table than him, but he had gained a few awkward-size freckles on his chin. This dating disaster was *all* his fault for always looking so damned good—even with paint freckles.

"Nice, Mill." He took a napkin from the holder she kept on the table. "Real mature."

"Oh—like you leaving me to deal with your date was mature?"

"For the last time, she wasn't my date. I only went along with this whole thing on the off chance I might get to spend more time with you."

"Please, don't do that."

"What?" Her heart fluttered just to witness a flash of his slow grin.

"Act like you care, when you obviously don't."

He leisurely rose, sauntering toward her with cowboy swagger.

Dear Lord...

"My problem—" he knelt alongside her, manhandling her chair until turning her far enough to face him "—is that I care too much. From the second I stepped back into this house, you've been all I can think of. I keep seeing flashes of you when we were kids and then older, in high school—back before you and Jim were even an item. How had I never noticed you? How had I let him get to you first? But then what kind of lowlife does that make me? If Jim were alive, he'd owe me an ass-kicking."

She licked her lips, willing her runaway pulse to slow. "That's the thing—he's not here. But we are. And that's got me so confused." *I want you more than I've ever wanted anything in my whole life.* But was that just her body talking? Or something more? How was she supposed to know?

He rose just high enough to kiss her, resting his hands on her thighs, singeing her tender flesh through her robe. "You taste so damned good."

He urged her mouth open, sweeping her tongue with his. An erotic jolt slammed through her, colliding flaming desire into an icy wall of guilt. Despite her speech, she still knew what they were doing was wrong, but that fact didn't even remotely slow them down.

When he took her hands, urging her from her chair, she let him, and when he dipped his kisses deep into her robe's open vee, she didn't offer the slightest protest. All that mattered was the velvety warmth centered between her legs and spreading like wicked syrup throughout every inch of her fevered body.

The house was quiet save for the clock ticking over the stove. Everyone had been sleeping for hours, which was why when Cooper untied her robe, instead of fighting him, she only held her breath, praying for release of the forbidden tension that'd been building ever since he'd come home.

He was kneeling again, worshipping her abdomen with kisses, skimming his hands along her hips, dragging down her panties until the room's chill touched her hot core.

Back to her lips, he kissed the breath from her, dizzying her from his urgency that surprisingly matched her own.

His slipping his finger inside her seemed the most natural thing in the world, as did his nipping her rock-hard nipple through her bra. He set a rhythm that left her alternately gasping and moaning, twining her arms round his neck for support, kissing him, kissing him until he made her come, moaning her pleasure into his mouth.

"More…" she begged. She was no longer a mom or

widow, but a woman. A woman desperate to once again feel alive in every sense of the word.

"Sure?"

Cheek pressed to the warm wall of his chest, she nodded.

And then he was shoving aside the paint and volcano to ease her back, leaving her for only the instant it took him to unfasten his jeans. He'd just touched his tip inside her, when he stopped.

"Wh-what's wrong?" she managed to say. He needed to keep going before she lost her nerve.

"I don't have protection."

"I don't care." And in the moment, she truly didn't.

It'd been so long, that the first few thrusts were painful. Tears sprung to her eyes, but then he slowed and kissed pain away, and then pleasure was once again building and spreading into a lavish labyrinth of stunning heat and joy and spiraling, ever-climbing, raw sensation. This man had somehow become her moon and stars and everything in between.

With his every thrust, she gripped his biceps harder, raising her hips, urging him deeper, deeper until she came again in a glorious Technicolor dream.

He rested on top of her, showering her with adoring kisses that only made her want him again. Was this normal? It'd been so long since she'd been with a man, she couldn't even remember. All she knew was that she wasn't sorry. Not one bit.

Though she probably would be in the morning…

SUNDAY MORNING, COOPER volunteered to help his dad eat breakfast. Considering what'd gone down in the kitchen the previous night, he wasn't sure he could ever again look at the table with a straight face.

"How are you?" Cooper asked, mixing butter and sugar into the oatmeal.

"T-tired."

"Me, too." He fed Clint his first bite. "I went on a date with your therapist. What's her name? Sandy? Sissy?"

"St-Stacie…"

"Yeah, that's it. Anyway, it was a rough night. She's a sweet girl, but not really my type. I guess when it comes down to it, if I ever settle down, I'd want a woman more like Millie. Someone who's not afraid to get her hands dirty, and isn't into all the fancy hair and makeup. I like an earthy girl, you know?"

His dad grunted then swallowed his latest bite.

"Truth is, I couldn't sleep a wink. Just thinking about things. Makes me crazy when that happens." He helped his dad with a few more spoonfuls then a few sips of coffee. "How come you couldn't sleep?"

Clint gestured for Cooper to hand over his whiteboard. He then wrote: *Too damned noisy!*

Cooper's stomach tightened. Did that mean what he thought it did? That his father hadn't been *out* when…

His cheeks felt hot enough to fry an egg. No, no, no.

"Too noisy, huh? What? Did you have an owl outside your window? Coyotes?"

Clint erased the board with his elbow, then wrote: *All that rutting!*

Cooper gulped. Okay, no biggie. No need to panic. He'd been trained in crisis management and thinking on his feet in the often-fluid situation of battle. "Geez, Dad,

I'm sorry. I'll bet you overheard the movie I was watching. Parts were pretty racy—if you know what I mean."

His father didn't look all that convinced.

"WHY DOES MY volcano look splotchy?"

Late Sunday morning, Millie took a sheet of oatmeal cookies from the oven, pretending she hadn't heard her daughter's embarrassing question.

"Mom? Did you hear me?"

Mortification didn't begin describing how awful Millie felt about not only the odd paint pattern on LeeAnn's science-fair project, but also for her own downright scandalous behavior. What had she been thinking? "I heard you, okay? I don't know how it happened. Maybe Cheetah's been on the table?"

As traitorous as that cat was, he deserved the blame!

"Yeah, I'll bet he did it…"

"Have fun at your party?" *Wish I hadn't had quite so much fun at mine.*

"Yeah, but Kara and Finleigh kept calling boys, and the boy I wanted to talk to was at his grandparents' and couldn't talk. I wish I knew if he liked me."

"What boy?" Since when had her baby girl even known boys existed?

"His name's Damon. He's in sixth grade, and his eyes are all dreamy, but I don't want him using them to look at any other girls."

Back up the truck. Though Millie would like nothing more than to dissect every possible meaning behind what'd transpired after she and Cooper had—well, fornicated, for lack of a better word—it sounded like her daughter needed her more.

"Honey…" She used a spatula to transfer the cookies from the sheet to a plate. "Don't you think you're a little young for boys?"

"No. God, Mom, Kara's had a boyfriend for like three months."

"Okay, first—when you say boyfriend, what exactly are we talking? Like you just talk at recess? And second—do Kara's parents know about this guy?"

LeeAnn rolled her eyes. "You're so lame."

"And you're a little too mouthy. And way too young to be even thinking about boys."

"What do you know about them? It's not like you ever date."

Touché. "How about you take a nice, long time-out up in your room."

"I have to work on my volcano."

"Write on the research paper that goes along with it."

As luck would have it, Cooper chose that moment to stroll through the back door. He wore faded work jeans, boots, an old, red flannel shirt and his raggedy straw hat. Despite all of that, he looked so handsome, Millie dropped a cookie on the floor. And then her mind's eye recalled what'd happened right there on the kitchen table, and she wanted to dissolve into a confused puddle.

LeeAnn shot her uncle a preteen stony glare then stomped off toward the hall.

Cheetah shot out from under the table, dragging the cookie to the utility porch. Weird, traitorous cat who apparently thought he was a dog.

"What's she in a snit about?" Peg asked on her way into the kitchen from doing Clint's physical therapy.

"Can you believe it? Boys." Millie glanced up to catch Cooper's mossy-green gaze. Just thinking about what they'd done made her nipples harden. It'd been filthy! But then afterward, he'd been so sweet, and then strangely distant—as if nothing had even happened.

"She's too young for that."

"Exactly." To avoid looking at Cooper, Millie focused on spooning dough onto the cookie sheet.

"Mom!" J.J. called from the living room, where they were watching a movie. "When are the cookies gonna be done? Me and Cayden are starving!"

"Just a minute!" Why, on the one morning when she really needed private time with Cooper to dissect what'd transpired between them was all hell-a-poppin' in the Hansen home?

Chapter Fourteen

"Pretty day, isn't it?"

"Yep." Cooper kept right on hammering. He didn't pause to admire how well Millie filled out her jeans, or how the sun glinted off the few red streaks in her hair. When he'd been in the kitchen—the scene of his crime—with her that morning, he couldn't escape fast enough.

Millie hung clothes on the line.

If not for the jet overhead bound for Denver International, they could have been in another century. Part of him wished they were. Lord knew, things would be less complicated. But then would they? All things being relative, nothing would change. He'd still have carried a wagonload of emotional baggage, and she'd still be his brother's widow.

"Looks like you're making good progress on the coop." She hung up a pint-size pair of jeans.

"Yep." He kept right on framing by fitting in a 2x4.

"You planning on avoiding me forever?"

Yep. "There's not much to say other than it shouldn't have happened. I shouldn't have let it."

"Did it ever occur to you that I'm half of this equation and wanted it to happen?"

He sighed. "Yeah, well, you shouldn't have. I'm no good, and you're like a saint. Raising two great kids, looking after my dad and the ranch. You're my brother's *wife*."

"Correction..." She hung a tiny T-shirt. And another and another until her motions looked frantic. "I *was* Jim's wife, but he left me. He was stupid—so stupid, to die like he did. It was a useless, senseless death that still makes me furious." Now she was crying, and the racking sobs shredded Cooper's heart. "How could he be so careless with his life?"

He set down his hammer and went to her—not caring who saw.

"I'm sorry." He kissed the crown of her head.

She pushed him away. "No. I don't want pity. I want you to view me not as Jim's wife, your sister-in-law, but as me—*Millie*. The girl who watched you at rodeos and thought you were the wildest thing I'd ever seen. Jim was wonderfully safe, he was my rock, but you were—are..."

Her teary smile rocked his world.

"*Amazing*. And I don't just mean—you know. I'm talking about how you've swept in here and made everything better. I could've maintained the status quo, but by you taking the ranch duties off my hands, I feel like I can breathe again. I can't thank you enough for that."

He tucked his hands in his pockets. "You're welcome, but about last night... It can't happen again."

"Because you're not attracted to me?" The tears streaming down her cheeks glistened in the sun. And that felt wrong. No one should be crying on such a gift of a February day—especially not a woman as gorgeous as Millie.

"Seriously?" He drew her back into his arms for a kiss, then tucked flyaway strands of her hair behind her ears. "Never doubt your beauty. You're stunning."

"No, I'm not. My nails are a mess and my hair's never done. I saw the girls you dated in high school, and I would never have been one of them."

"Are we in high school?" He brushed his thumb over her full lower lip then leaned in for a nibble. "I sure as hell hope not, because then I wouldn't be able to do this…" He kissed her nice and slow, knowing the whole while he shouldn't, but what kind of man would he be to let a woman as perfect as she was spend one more moment crying?

Her breathy mew made him hard as hell. "Thought we weren't doing this anymore?"

"We're not. This really is the last time, okay?"

She returned his kiss, this time with a bad-girl hint of tongue. "Yes. That's probably best."

"No more insecurities, okay?" He tucked his hand under her chin, directing her gaze to his. "Promise?"

She nodded.

"Good girl." He kissed her forehead. The tip of her nose. He wanted to journey farther, but held strong in his resolve to keep his roving hands to himself. Their table *tango* never should've happened. She deserved better than that, than him.

SUNDAY AFTERNOON, MILLIE stood alongside Peg's compact car while she rearranged the contents of her overstuffed trunk in an attempt to close it. "Why don't you take out your toiletry case and put it in the backseat?"

"Because I've got all my quilting gear there. I finished a whole section while you and my brother were off partying."

"Whoa—don't you mean your brother and Stacie?" Because it was the God's honest truth that Millie hadn't enjoyed a lick of what'd gone on down at Mack's. And after? There went the annoying heat in her cheeks. Well, after had been a whole other story.

"Cut the act. I saw you two kissing out back today."

"You were spying on us?"

"I was washing dishes and happened to look out the window behind the sink. What if it'd been LeeAnn or J.J. who saw? Spill it. What's going on between you two?"

"We kissed, but it was no big deal. We both agreed it was a mistake. End of story."

"I don't think so. Do you feel something special for him? If so, when did you know? Is he quitting the Navy to stay here or still leaving, because I can't imagine you and the kids following him."

"Peg, stop." Millie looked over her shoulder to make sure they were still alone. "Even if I knew the answers to all of those questions, I don't think I'd tell you. What-ever's going on is complicated and—I'm sure in the grand scheme of things—nothing important. Just two lonely people sharing a moment."

"You two don't just have shared moments, Mill, but a long history. Think about it. You crushed on Cooper long before realizing Jim was the more stable of the two Hansen boys."

"Ha!" Millie hugged herself in twilight's growing chill. "What a crock that turned out to be. Hopefully, even Cooper's not stupid enough to stand up on a mov-ing four-wheeler while shooting."

Peg sighed. "You ever going to forgive him?"

Millie crossed her arms. "Nope."

"Okay, well, for the record, I think you could do worse in men than Cooper. I'm beyond thrilled to see him and Dad getting along. Would it really be so awful for you to end up with another Hansen man?"

"Okay, wait—we shared a kiss, and already you're marrying us off?"

"Think about it. He's a ready-made dad and ranch hand. You could—and have—gone years without meeting another candidate as suitable as him." Peg tossed the toiletry bag on top of her quilting gear then slammed the trunk closed. "Just sayin'."

THURSDAY AFTERNOON WHILE cutting trash bags to protect LeeAnn's volcano from the light snow, Millie still couldn't get Peg's words out of her head.

Last week at this time, if someone had told her she'd have used a man for his body, she'd have laughed them out of the county, but in hindsight, had that essentially been what happened between her and Cooper? If Peg knew the whole truth, she'd freak.

Every time Millie relived what she and Cooper had done on this very table, her stomach flipped—only in a good way—wishing she had the courage to do it again.

"Mom?" LeeAnn asked. "Have you seen my report?"

"It's in your blue folder on top of the printer."

"Thanks."

"Can I have ice cream for dinner?" J.J. asked from in front of the freezer.

"No. Once we help your sister set up her project, we might have time to go out for dinner during the judging. We'll have to play it by ear."

"But I thought the science fair was tomorrow?"

"It is, but judges go through tonight to decide who won. Then tomorrow, all the people visiting the fair will be able to see the winners."

J.J. cocked his head. "I don't get it."

"Me, neither, bud." Cooper sauntered in from Clint's room, where he'd been helping his father eat.

No matter how many times Millie told herself she was over him, his striking profile never failed to send her pulse into a gallop.

Cooper grabbed a banana from the counter fruit bowl, snapped it in half, and gave part to her son. He then took a piece of bologna from the fridge, ate three-quarters and fed the rest to Cheetah, who rubbed against his ankles. Maybe that's how he got the cat to like him. Bribes! "How about we let your mom and LeeAnn just tell us where we need to be and when?"

"Yeah, that sounds good." J.J. looked to Cooper in awe.

"If I'm in charge—" Millie duct-taped the last trash bag in place "—then how about you two put on clean shirts? And one of you probably needs to wash your face."

"Oops, that's me," Cooper teased.

Even if it was meant for her son, Millie couldn't get enough of her brother-in-law's smile. Since their talk in the backyard, though she wouldn't even try denying the sexual tension, there'd also been a lightness between them she found irresistible. He was also getting along great with J.J. and Clint. LeeAnn, however, still merely tolerated him—even after he'd printed his Mount Vesuvius and Pompeii pictures for her and helped with her project's eruption.

What if Peg was right? That Cooper truly was the guy she was meant to rebuild her life with? Only her insecurities and doubts caused them to miss their opportunity?

The question haunted her while loading everyone and LeeAnn's volcano into the truck, and more still while thanking Lynette for watching Clint while they'd be gone.

By the time Cooper had driven them to town, her mind felt messy. Once they'd all made two treks from the truck into the school through heavy snow with the various parts of LeeAnn's project, while J.J. ran around with found friends, Millie led Cooper to a seat on the gym's bleachers.

"Shouldn't we be helping her assemble everything?" he asked.

"Nope. She'd be disqualified."

"What if she doesn't remember where to put all the tubing?"

Millie cast him a sideways smile. "Relax. And welcome to being an uncle."

"Thanks." After returning her smile, he nudged her shoulder with his. He'd no doubt meant the gesture as friendly, so why did her whole body tingle? "All the uncle manuals skip this part—about wanting your niece to beat the crap out of every other kid in a purely scientific manner."

"Oh, of course." She laughed and nodded.

Other parents joined them in the stands until the school principal herded them all into the cafeteria to await the announcement of the winners.

"You know," Cooper said between bites of the chocolate cake the PTA moms had provided—turned out there hadn't been time for dinner, "though I saw a few other volcanoes, Lee clearly had the most complex."

"Absolutely."

Was it wrong that she found so much joy in once again coparenting? Cooper might technically only be her children's uncle, but she remembered Jim being every bit as competitive when it came to their kids' winning.

Even better? Not standing around alone while groups of moms and dads gathered. She'd grown weary of always being on her own. Before his stroke, Clint had tagged along whenever he could, but it'd never been the same.

Forty minutes and three pieces of cake later, Cooper asked, "How long does it take to determine Lee's the winner?"

"In my experience, whether you're waiting for a riding lesson to end or tutoring or Little League, it always takes around ten minutes longer than you feel you can stand waiting without a mental breakdown."

"Good to know," he said with a nod. "I'm damn near there."

Twenty minutes later, winners were finally named.

When LeeAnn came in third in her age group to a robot that dunked cookies in milk and a tsunami machine, Cooper was outraged.

"What the hell?" he asked under his breath. "There's no way that scrawny kid made that robotic arm all on his own. Look at the way his dad's beaming—clear case of cheating to me. That guy probably works for NASA."

Millie grimaced. "Maybe, but another *uncling* tip for you is that despite how much you want to pitch a fit about any number of injustices toward one's child, we must always be gracious and follow the adage of catching more flies with honey than vinegar."

"That's bullshit."

She elbowed him. "Another rule? Even though you're a grown-up, you still can't cuss at school."

Sighing, he shook his head. "No wonder I was glad to get out of this place. Too damned many rules."

He got it again with her elbow. "I'm starving. Let's find the kids and get out of here."

"Yes, ma'am. Want to divide and conquer? I'll grab the munchkin and you find Lee?"

"Sounds like a plan." Yet another benefit of coparenting—not having to track down both kids by herself.

Watching Cooper's broad shoulders easily part through the crowd, Millie fully realized just how weary she'd grown of being a single parent. But that realization was a long way from promoting Cooper from uncle to dad.

J.J. STILL SLEPT with a night-light, so Cooper couldn't help but wonder why he'd ventured so far down a dark school hall.

A metallic clang, then giggle, came from about fifty feet in front of Cooper's current location, and he was guessing by the sounds' slight diffusion, down another hall to the left. Sure enough, he soon had to make another turn into a new addition that hadn't been here when he'd attended this school.

He heard another giggle.

Saw a couple kissing in the faint light eking in from the snow-covered parking lot.

Cooper cleared his throat. "Excuse me. Either one

of you seen— Are you freakin' kidding me?" His eyes narrowed. "LeeAnn?"

"Don't tell Mom."

"You—" Cooper pointed to the boy "—get the hell away from my niece."

The kid took one look at the same game face Cooper used when taking down terrorists and shot off toward the cafeteria.

"God—" LeeAnn straightened her long pigtails "—did you have to be so scary?"

"You're both lucky I didn't do worse. Your mom, on the other hand, is going to blow bigger than your volcano."

"*Please,* don't tell her."

Arms crossed, he asked, "Give me one good reason why I shouldn't."

"With Grandpa Clint's stroke and all the bills she's always worrying about, I don't want her worrying about me. I promise, I'll never kiss Damon again."

Damon? Coincidence that the kid's name was only one letter off from demon? Though Cooper hated to admit it, his niece had made a valid point. Millie did have a lot on her plate—considering what'd gone down Saturday night, even more than her daughter knew. Besides, since LeeAnn promised not to kiss the kid again, if Cooper did let it slide, then would she maybe cut him some slack and quit avoiding him like he had an infectious disease?

"Please, Uncle Cooper. I pinkie swear I won't even talk to him again. *Please,* don't tell Mom."

"All right," he said, "but I never want to catch you with that kid again."

BY THE TIME all four of them trudged back out to Cooper's truck, three inches of snow coated the windshield.

Millie hoped the roads would be clear enough by the next afternoon for Peg to make her usual weekend trip to see Clint.

Her evening with Cooper had been alarmingly pleasant, and she looked forward to his sister being around to chaperone, because honestly? As charming as he'd been tonight, she didn't trust herself to keep her hands off him.

He started the engine, then said to J.J., "Bud, you wanna help me clear windows?"

"I can't reach."

"That's what I'm for…"

"Cool! Piggyback me, Uncle Cooper!"

After her son bounced his way out of the truck, Millie angled on the front seat to get a better view of her daughter. "I'm proud of you. There were a lot of great projects."

LeeAnn shrugged. "I did okay, but only the first two in each category go to the regional science fair."

Millie patted LeeAnn's forearm. "Whenever that's supposed to be, we'll go do something fun. Next year, we won't make just a robotic arm, but a whole robot, okay?"

LeeAnn nodded, but still seemed down.

"Sweetie, don't sweat it. I'm super impressed by how hard you've worked. You should be proud, too."

J.J. banged on the window. *"Mom! Look at me!"*

Cooper had set him on the hood, where he was now standing while brushing snow from the windshield.

"Get him down from there!" Millie waved to get Cooper's attention, but it wouldn't have mattered, as he'd already done her bidding, and the two guys were climbing back in the truck.

"That was fun!" J.J. was still bouncing.

"How much cake did you eat?" she asked her son.

"I dunno. I think lots!"

"Sounds about right…"

Because of the snow, they opted to skip going out for dinner in favor of driving straight home. By the time they reached the house, at least another couple of inches of snow had fallen.

J.J. was asleep, so Cooper carried him in.

LeeAnn bounded past Millie to beat all of them to the front door. Once inside, she hollered good-night, then darted up the stairs to her room.

"Poor thing." Millie hung her coat and hat on the hook by the door. "She's really taking her loss hard."

"She'll get over it." For him to be the same guy who was angered by the fact that LeeAnn's project hadn't placed higher, Cooper didn't seem all that upset.

"I suppose."

"Want me to put him to bed?" Cooper kissed J.J.'s temple.

"Yes, please." His simple, sweet gesture toward her son tightened Millie's chest, making it hard to breathe. More every day, she cherished Cooper's connection to her kids. Tonight, he'd even somehow managed to find LeeAnn before her.

"Hey…" Lynette wandered in from the living room. "I was starting to worry about you guys. It's looking bad out there."

"We got behind a plow on the main road, so it wasn't too dicey. You'll probably want to be in four-wheel-drive for your trip home, though."

"I figured as much." She put a bookmark in the paperback she'd been reading.

"Want Cooper to drive you?"

"Thanks, but I've been dealing with this crap for a while. I'll be fine." Her friend waved off her concern much the way she had when Millie had taken off mad on Valentine's Day. They'd been friends since grade school, and no matter the tussle, it never took long for them to repair any damage.

Lynette agreed to call when she was safely home, then Millie saw her out the front door.

Cooper strode back down the stairs. "I'm going to check on Dad."

"Okay. You hungry? I was thinking about scrambling some eggs."

"Sounds good." He paused with his hand on the newel post.

"You all right?"

"Sure. Fine." His dour expression didn't match his words.

She eyed him for a few long seconds. "Lee's loss is weighing heavy on you, too, huh?"

He ducked his gaze. "I guess so."

"It's all right." Though she knew better than to touch him, she smoothed her hand up and down his back. His wool pea jacket was damp from snow, but this close and personal, she caught a whiff of his leathery aftershave and nearly drowned in contentment. Did he have to be so perfect in darn near every way? "Now that you're back in the kids' lives, there will be plenty more science fairs. You're more than welcome to help with every single one."

His faint smile faded. "Wish I'd be here, but from Virginia to Colorado is an awfully long ride."

"True," she conceded, "but we're worth it, don't you think?" The moment the words left her mouth, she regretted them.

The last thing she wanted was for him to for one second believe she wanted him to stay, because knowing Cooper and his newfound sense of family duty, he might just do it out of obligation.

When—*if*—she ever did enter into another committed relationship, she wanted it to be because he loved her, not because he felt sorry for her.

Chapter Fifteen

A week later, Cooper was glad for Zane's help in raising the walls and putting the roof joists on Millie's chicken coop. Right now it was just a shell, but he remembered what she'd told him about wanting her birds to live in a fancy abode. Ever since, Cooper had been stuck on the idea of making her wildest chicken coop fantasy come true.

If only I could work on a few of her other fantasies....

It was nice being around his old school friend and rodeo buddy. The two of them had shared good times. Plus, having company helped Cooper's mind from straying to Millie and the alarming amount of moments he spent wishing they could be together.

By the time they'd installed the fourth and final roof brace, Zane collapsed onto the hard-packed ground. "Are you trying to kill me? How the hell do you have so much energy?"

Cooper laughed. "Clean living, my friend."

"Bullshit. When we meet up at Mack's, you put a beer back just as fast as the rest of our old crew. Come on, what's your secret?"

"If I had to guess, I'd say it's my workout."

"Where are you hitting a gym around here?"

Cooper laughed. "You don't need a gym, man. It's all in here." He tapped his temple. "Run, do a few dozen pull-ups from one of the lower barn rafters. No big deal. If you want, meet me in the morning around five. I'll take you through my drill."

MARCH 1, MILLIE sat in the home office, staring at a fresh pile of bills. So much around the place had changed, yet still more hadn't. She didn't tell Cooper about their financial problems, not because they were embarrassing, but because she knew once they culled the herd in late May, that they'd make enough to pay almost everything. In the meantime, she'd just have to keep juggling her available funds.

The kids got Jim's social security check, but that barely covered the basics. Clint also had social security, but his money had all been funneled into paying for his medical costs.

Cooper knocked on the open door. "Are you using the computer?"

"No. Go ahead." She scooped up her bill pile and set them on a side table across the room. "What are you going to do?"

"Since Dad and J.J. are finally occupied with a movie, I thought I'd answer a few emails and research my project." He winked. "My iPad's dead, and on the charger."

"Sure. Sounds good." She fought to maintain her composure. Ever since what he now called their *lapse in judgment,* he'd grown faultlessly, disgustingly polite. She missed their sometimes heated banter. Even more, she missed their few stolen kisses.

His project was rebuilding the chicken coop, but he

was being so hush-hush about it that he'd gone so far as to string sheets across part of the yard so she couldn't see the structure from the kitchen sink window. He spent so much time out there, she couldn't imagine what it would look like. She'd told him about once admiring a fancy coop. Had he listened and was now breathing life into what she'd only meant as a casual statement?

The fact that he'd truly listened to her bit of small talk warmed her through and through. It had to be significant, right?

"Need me to get you anything?" she asked.

"No, thank you." He'd already opened an email.

"Okay, well, I'll leave you to it." What was wrong with him? How could he stand them being in the same room and not at least sharing a touch?

In a perfect world, he'd have entered the room and kissed her, maybe given her knotted shoulders a rub. They'd have shared their days and maybe wandered into the kitchen for cocoa and a slice of the cherry pie she'd made for that night's dessert.

"You all right?" He stopped typing to glance her way. Just the sight of his mossy-green stare was enough to make her knees weak. How did he maintain his composure? Or, like she suspected, was he just not that into her and his polite speech out by the clothesline had been his way of letting her down easy? "You look washed out."

"Thanks. That's the nicest thing anyone's said to me all week."

"Aw, I didn't mean it in a bad way. Just that you look tired. Why don't you have a nice long soak, then go to bed. I'll make sure everyone else is tucked in."

"You'd do that?" As much as she cherished bedtime rituals with J.J. and LeeAnn, the thought of letting Cooper assume all of her duties while she essentially pampered herself was too good of an opportunity to pass up.

"Sure. It's no problem." He didn't even look up from reading his letter. But then what had she expected? For him to sweep her into his arms, making her promise to add extra rose oil to her bathwater so her skin smelled nice when he snuggled alongside her in bed?

Her traitorous pulse raced at the possibilities of what else they might do in her bed.

"Go on," he said. "You're wasting valuable tub time."

Mouth dry from holding back all the things she wanted to say to him, but shouldn't, Millie visually drank him in once more then trudged upstairs to draw her water.

Once she'd submerged herself beneath fragrant bubbles and closed her eyes, she'd anticipated peace.

What she got were memories of their wild night in the kitchen that were hot enough to bring her bath water to a boil!

NEXT WEDNESDAY, COOPER parked at the feed store's side door, killed the truck's engine then sighed. Millie sat alongside him. More than anything, he wanted to kiss her, but he fought the temptation.

The sky was gray, snow tumbled in halfhearted flurries and the temperature was a balmy ten degrees. As if checking the herd in this weather hadn't been enough fun, before she'd left for school, he'd caught LeeAnn on her mom's cell with that Damon kid—he knew, because he'd redialed the number. What was the protocol on this sort of thing? His niece had promised to never kiss the kid again, but should Cooper have extended that promise to include cutting all contact? But then how was that even possible when they'd see each other at school?

He asked, "Doesn't this town depress the hell out of you?"

"Wait until spring. Everything will look better."

"How?" The same planters filled with dead plants still hung from the street's ornamental light posts, and more storefronts were empty than filled. Weeds grew through sidewalk cracks, and there were more mounds of dirty snow than cars.

"What do you mean? You don't remember spring? The way everything greens up and the blue sky looks big enough for you to fly right into—" she grinned "—assuming you had wings."

"Right. There is that." *Lord, I want to kiss you.*

"You know what I mean. Yes, this winter has been especially nasty, but you'll see. Once May rolls around, this place is going to be looking mighty tempting. So tempting in fact, you might never want to leave."

He snorted. "You been sniffing J.J.'s school paste?" *The sooner I hit the road, the better.* Being around her was dangerous. She made him want the family he didn't deserve.

She answered his question with a dirty look. "In all seriousness, before you came, I didn't hold out much hope for this place. I figured by spring we'd have lost the ranch and moved into a Denver apartment. Now…" Her wide-eyed look of gratitude made up for what the hiding sun couldn't. "For the first time in forever— knock on wood—I think everything might be okay."

Cooper wished he shared her optimism, but even if they made a boatload of cash at the cattle auction, he wasn't naive, and had seen her bills. They could sell the entire herd, and it wouldn't be enough to put the ranch on the solid foundation he wanted for her, his dad and the kids.

"COME OUTSIDE. AND close your eyes." Since both kids were still at school, Cooper took Millie's hand to guide her out to the backyard on the deceptively sunny mid-March day. Though it was bright, the air still held a nip from the previous night's sleet, meaning the sheet he'd hung to stop Millie from eyeing her surprise through the kitchen window had been frozen to the clothesline. "Oh—and put this on."

He took her long sweater from the back-door hook, holding it out for her to slip her arms through, wishing that when their arms accidentally brushed, his attraction for her hadn't felt more like pain. But then what was the point in lying? He honestly wanted her so bad, it hurt.

"How am I going to see?"

He took her hand. "Let me guide you."

Ever since learning of her wish for a fancy home in which to house her chickens, he'd been consumed with the idea to surprise her. For weeks, he'd toiled to make every part perfect, right down to planting pansies in the wide front porch's flower boxes.

During their morning workouts, Zane had come straight out and told him he was crazy for putting so much time, money and energy into this kind of nutty venture, but Cooper didn't care. He was crazy, all right.

Crazy about his brother's wife.

He'd do damn near anything for her. Anything, but tie her down to a misfit like himself.

"Are we almost there?" She tripped over an exposed

tree root, but he caught her. Touching her and not kissing her proved a lesson in restraint.

"A little farther." The phrase also applied to how
much he alternately looked forward to and dreaded leaving. His dad grew stronger by the day, which meant
Cooper's time on the ranch was almost done. He led
Millie past the clothesline and around the cottonwood.
Upon reaching their destination, he forced a deep
breath, wishing her reaction to his big reveal didn't
mean so much. "Okay, open your eyes."

She gasped then covered her mouth with her hands.
"Cooper, it's…" Her eyes welled.

"What's that mean? Are you happy? Sad?" If she
didn't like what he'd done, though it might sound silly to
anyone else, he'd be crushed. He'd poured himself into
this project, heart and soul. What emotion he couldn't
give to her, he'd given to the damn chickens. Stupid,
but there it was.

"I'm…" She laughed through tears then damn near
toppled him with a hug. "I'm so happy! This is stunning—you really did build me the Taj Mahal of chicken
coops."

He sharply exhaled. *She likes it.*

Gratitude flowed through him, making him feel like
a second-grader basking in his teacher's approval. But
over the past couple of months, Millie had come to mean
the world to him. Her opinion mattered.

"I'm in awe…" She gingerly stepped onto the front
porch, laughing when she tried out the swing. Every
inch of the coop had been covered in Victorian-era swag
he'd painted in a half-dozen purple shades, ranging from
lavender to deep violet.

"How can I ever thank you?"

You already did with your smile. "I'm good."

She opened the door slowly and with reverence. The inside smelled of new lumber, straw and grain. Under the heat lamps' glow, Millie's chickens gurgled and clucked in contentment. Golden sun warmed the floor through a skylight.

"This is almost too nice for just the chickens." She wiped tears from her cheeks. "It's amazing. Better than I'd even imagined."

"Good. Mission accomplished." But if that was truly the case, why was he already feeling empty inside? Like he needed another grand gesture to make Millie see how much he cared?

MARCH PASSED, AND then somehow it was Easter Sunday in late April. Just as Millie had predicted to Cooper on that frigid day in March, the high prairie had sprung back to life—much like her, only in a way she couldn't in a million years have predicted.

She was pregnant.

The fact alternately terrified and thrilled her.

On the terror side, right along with wondering how they'd ever financially manage with another mouth to feed and what her friends and neighbors would think of her having an unplanned baby she'd conceived with her brother-in-law, came the bonus worry of when she should tell Cooper her news.

By now, she knew him well enough to guess that once he learned he'd soon be a dad, he'd go all noble cowboy on her, demanding they march down to the courthouse for a wedding. But was that what she really wanted?

Make no mistake, with every part of her being, she

wished he'd stay, but not out of a sense of obligation—because he felt trapped. Sure, tongues would wag, but gossips would soon enough find something else to occupy their chatter.

On the bright side, just as she'd never felt more healthy and vibrantly alive than when carrying Lee-Ann and J.J., this pregnancy was proving the same. Colors and smells seemed more vivid, and her heart swelled with an overall sense of well-being. This baby was a gift. Her proof that even after suffering through her loss of Jim, life didn't just have to soldier on, but sometimes it skipped while humming a happy tune.

While putting the finishing touches on the lamb cake she'd made for their annual after-church picnic, Millie allowed herself to daydream of Cooper's reaction to learning her news. Would he be elated? Confess his love and then pamper her right up to holding her hand through the delivery? Or would he feel bitter and trapped, wishing he'd never set foot back in his hometown?

The last thought made her queasy, so she downed a few saltines and ginger ale.

"You look pretty."

"Thanks." She glanced up to find Cooper leaning against the kitchen pass-through. He was so handsome, he took her breath away. If he wasn't happy about their baby, she wasn't sure how she'd cope. She guessed the same way she always had, dowsing her dreams with the hard work and even harder realities of living as a single mom on a working ranch.

Tell him, her heart urged, but her dry mouth strangely failed to work.

"Where is everyone?" His hair was still damp from a

shower. Even from ten feet away, she smelled his leathery aftershave and wanted to rest her cheek against his chest, just breathing him in.

"Peg's outside with the kids, setting up tables in the yard. Thanks to the wheelchair ramp you built, Clint's with them—no doubt, barking orders."

Cooper laughed.

Since it wasn't a sound she heard often, Millie relished the moment.

"It's good seeing him up. His physical therapist said he should be walking under his own steam with just a cane by the end of the month."

"Thank goodness. His mood sure has improved since he's not always stuck in bed."

"Can you blame him?" Cooper sat at the table. The same table Millie still couldn't look at without blushing. "This is off topic, but I know you plan on culling the herd in the next month or two, and I did some research and found a company that does live internet auctions. That saves the stress on our stock of having to travel— except to their new home."

"Okay…" Since her pregnancy test had turned out positive, Millie hadn't even thought about the auction. But she needed to. The bills wouldn't pay themselves.

"Want me to set something up?"

"For when?" Because to her, culling the herd was synonymous with Cooper leaving.

"I was thinking about this time next month. That sound all right to you? Dad should be well enough to drive his four-wheeler by then. Plus, I'll move the rest of the herd to the north pasture. It's the closest and has easy access."

She only nodded, because she wasn't capable of

more. So this was it? He had his escape plan in place and was good to go?

"If you think that's too soon, say the word and we can put it off. But my CO's wanting me back on base, and I'm sure you and the kids are ready to get the house back to yourselves."

Tell him! "Yep. You've got that right."

"Then I'll set everything up. You won't have to do anything but cash the check."

And raise our child and nurse my broken heart.

COOPER KNEW HE was chewing Easter ham, but it tasted more like cardboard than brown-sugar glaze and cloves. He didn't fault the cook, but his own dour mood.

It didn't matter that the sun was shining and the temperature was T-shirt warm. Or that seated around this table was all of the family he had left in the world. Clint, Millie, J.J. and LeeAnn. His longtime friends Lynette and Zane. Even their closest neighbor, Mack, and his new bride, Wilma.

With his dad well on the way to a full recovery, all should've been right in Cooper's world. Even the calf he'd rescued had been weaned and now fit right in with the rest of the herd. Life should've been good. So how come ever since his talk with Millie about the cattle auction, he'd gotten the impression that she'd just as soon spit on him than look at him?

"Millie, d-dear, you d-did a fine job, but I'd like to say an ex-tra blessing." Though shaky, with Peg's help, Clint stood. His words spilled too fast and slurred, but he was unrecognizable from the broken man he'd been when Cooper had first arrived. "Th-thank you, Lord, for r-restoring my health, and f-for bringing home my son. A-men."

"Amen," all assembled said in unison.

Last year at this time, Cooper had been en route to Afghanistan. Back then, he never would've dreamed he'd hear his dad actually thank God for his being there, but now that he had, the thought of once again leaving brought on a mixed bag of emotions.

More than anything, he wanted to leave, but not for a logical reason. The truth was that the emotional bonds he'd formed with Millie and her kids and renewed with his father were still too fragile and new to trust. Were they even real? Now that Clint's crisis had passed, would he morph back into the belligerent son of a bitch he'd been when he kicked Cooper off the family land?

"Uncle Cooper, look! I'm a walrus!" J.J. held a couple of asparagus *tusks* to his mouth.

Cooper feigned lurching back in fright. "You're scary, bud. Don't bite me."

J.J. growled and chomped until Millie scolded him to mind his manners.

After the meal, while the kids played with Nerf guns the Easter bunny had brought along with too much chocolate, Peg, Wilma and Lynette talked about *The Young and the Restless,* and Clint, Zane and Mack recalled their favorite elk-hunting stories.

Cooper excused himself from the crowd, finding Millie on the front porch swing. "Care for company?"

She scooted over.

"You were awfully quiet at dinner."

"I could say the same about you."

"I s'pose." A soft, warm breeze rustled the tree leaves and tall grasses at the yard's edge.

Their thighs and hips and shoulders touched on the cramped swing. The resulting hum of attraction made it hard for him to think. Couldn't she feel it, too?

After a few minutes of shared silence, Millie asked, "Does it look like Zane has lost weight to you?"

"Yeah. He's looking good." Their morning workouts were paying off so well that a couple of their other old high school friends were following what Zane called his SEAL Sessions.

"Coop?" She angled to face him. "What do you think about kids?"

"You mean your kids, or kids in general?"

"In general."

He furrowed his forehead. "Well, the couples I know with babies always look exhausted, and the ones with school-age kids don't fare much better. I shudder to think how much trouble teens would be. The whole parenting thing sounds like a nightmare—not that J.J. and Lee aren't great, because they are. But with them, you and Jim already did the heavy lifting. I imagine starting from scratch would be a bitch."

She winced.

"I'm not sure how you and Jim did it."

"Yeah… It was rough." Her complexion paled.

"What's with the questions? Someone you know expecting?"

Chapter Sixteen

That night, Millie sat on her bedroom's window seat, munching Oreos and trying to read, only her eyes didn't see to focus through tears.

Could Cooper have made himself any more clear? He didn't want a baby. And she just happened to be having his. Where did that leave her? What was she supposed to do?

She'd come close to confiding in Lynette and Peg, but couldn't. If her past pregnancies were any indication, by this time next month, she'd already be showing. She could play it off as a stress-eating weight gain for a little while, but eventually, the truth was literally going to pop out.

Millie put down her book to pace, but someone knocked on her closed door.

"Come in," she said, expecting LeeAnn or J.J.

"Hey." Cooper popped his head through the open door. "You decent?"

"Why wouldn't I be?"

"You never know. You being one of those quiet, good-girl types, your closet might be filled with male strippers." The fact that he said this with a straight face made her blood boil.

"Why are you here?" *Standing at my bedroom door, in my house, in my state?*

"Since your light was still on, I wanted to tell you how much I enjoyed your potato salad."

"My *potato salad?*" This whole conversation struck her as absurd. *I'm pregnant with your baby!* she wanted to scream. Instead, she demurely swept flyaway curls back into her ponytail. "Want the recipe?"

He furrowed his eyebrows. "What would I do with that? You know I don't cook."

"Just like you don't do kids?" The statement was petty and beneath her. So why had she said it? Maybe because she wanted so desperately to tell him about their baby, but was so afraid he'd have a negative reaction that she didn't dare.

"What's that supposed to mean?"

"Nothing. I'm sorry."

"No—you said it, so explain it." He shut the door, in the process, stealing all the oxygen from the room. It didn't matter that the night was warm and her window was open to a light breeze. He stood there larger than life, making her heart and mind spin like a child's top.

"I was referring to the comments you made when we were out on the porch swing. You made it plain you have no desire to be a father."

"So what? Why would that affect you?" Great question. One she had a very good answer for. *Tell him!*

"It doesn't, all right? Sorry I said anything."

Eyes narrowed, he asked, "What's going on with you, Mill? I thought we were in a good place. Am I missing something?"

Only everything! "I'm really tired. Do we have to do this now?"

"As far as I'm concerned, we don't have to do it ever. After the auction, I'll be gone. Your life will be back to normal, just as if I'd never even been here."

Only he had. And even though his time with them had been short, she remembered everything. Living with the chickens in the kitchen and bathing their newborn calf. The accidental kiss in the Red Lobster parking lot. Sharing intimate family moments like their special Valentine's Day breakfast. Being part of Clint's battle to regain his faculties. The wondrous chicken coop he'd built. Memories upon memories dulled her focus. She needed to remain strong in her resolve to not make him feel trapped into staying. If they were to ever share a true relationship based upon mutual love and respect, he had to come to her of his own free will—not a sense of obligation.

Tuesday, Cooper sat at the end of the old pond dock he and Jim had built with their father back when they'd both been in grade school. The day was fine with endless blue sky and a dazzling front range view.

He'd set up Clint in an outdoor canvas chair, handing him an already-baited, old-school cane pole that allowed for minimum work and maximum relaxation.

"I never thought I'd fish a-again…."

"I'm glad you're okay. You gave me a scare."

His dad grunted. "I scared m-myself."

The spring-fed pond's surface was glassy, giving them a clear view of the rocky bottom. The warm weather had brought out mayflies that flew in lazy patterns, every so often gliding too close to the water, only to then become fish food.

"I've missed this," Cooper said after dropping his

own line in the water. There was so much left unsaid
between them, but Clint had never been a big talker.
Maybe it was a guy thing, but most of Cooper's favorite times with his father had been when they were
alone, somehow speaking volumes without saying anything at all.

"You g-gonna marry her?"

"Huh?" Where had that come from? "You talking
about Millie?"

His old man nodded. "Sh-she's a good g-girl."

"I think so, too, but that doesn't mean I'd marry her.
Where in the world would you get an idea like that?"
A beauty of a rainbow trout nibbled at his line, but
darted away.

"S-seen you two t-together. Look g-good."

"Thanks, but that doesn't mean we're marriage material." Bedroom material? That was a whole other story.
They might've only shared one night, but it'd been beyond hot. What he wouldn't give to try again—only
this time in a proper bed.

"Th-think about it."

"I will," Cooper said, "but don't you think that'd be
a little odd? Me picking up where Jim left off?"

"Sh-she needs a good man. Th-that's what you have
b-become."

Cooper's eyes stung.

How long had he craved hearing exactly that from
his father? But when it came to the chemistry he shared
with Millie, her opinion was the only one that mattered.
Lately, they'd gotten along about as well as a pillowcase
filled with wet cats. He didn't know what he'd done to
piss her off, but apparently, it must've been major.

"WAIT—COULD YOU please say that again? I'm sure I didn't hear you right. There's probably a bad connection." Friday afternoon, Millie stood in the kitchen on the phone with the principal of LeeAnn's school, glaring at her gorgeous chicken coop, wishing anyone but Cooper had built it for her. That way, she wouldn't have to think nice things about him every time she gathered eggs.

"Mrs. Hansen, your daughter was caught in a compromising situation with a fellow student. We have rules against this, and she's received a week's worth of after-school detention. Because she rides the bus, that means you'll need to pick her up each day."

Holding her free hand to her suddenly pounding forehead, Millie forced a deep breath. "You must be mistaken. LeeAnn doesn't even talk to boys. I'll of course leave right away to pick her up, but this just can't be right."

"I realize news of this nature must be difficult to hear, Mrs. Hansen, but our security guard has video footage. Your daughter's identity is unmistakable."

After hanging up, Millie was so scattered, she couldn't even find her keys.

"What's up?" Cooper asked when she continued her search in the office. He sat at the computer, answering emails.

Clint napped in a nearby armchair with his feet up on the matching ottoman.

"I just got the craziest call from LeeAnn's school, and it has me rattled. The principal said she was caught in a compromising position with a boy. What does that even mean?" She looked under a magazine pile with no luck. "LeeAnn doesn't even talk to boys, but he said they've got video proof. Anyway, I have to get over to the school to pick her up and get this whole thing straightened out."

"Go w-with her," a groggy Clint barked from his corner.

Millie shook her head. "Cooper, you should stay here in case your father needs anything. Plus, someone needs to be here when J.J. gets home."

"*I* can w-watch him," Clint said. "Not *in-val-id.*"

"I know," she said to her father-in-law, "but if you're watching J.J., who's going to watch you?"

"She makes a good point." Cooper shut down the desktop unit.

"G-go w-with her," Clint insisted. "M-Millie too upset to d-drive."

"Mill?" Cooper asked from his perch on the edge of the desk. "What do you think?"

She pressed her fingers to her pounding temples. Though she'd never needed Cooper more, in light of her pregnancy, she didn't want to lean on him. She needed to be strong enough that when he left, she felt capable of carrying on. That said, he wasn't gone yet. Would it be so awful to accept his help one last time?

"All right," she finally answered, but mostly because she feared that without another adult present, if it turned out her precious baby girl truly had done what the principal accused her of, then Millie just might lose what little remained of her cool.

SEATED IN THE principal's office alongside Cooper, never had Millie been more grateful for his presence. He'd been a rock for her on the long trip into town, repeatedly assuring her everything would be okay until she'd almost believed he was right.

But that had been before Principal Conroy turned his computer monitor around so they could all see the alleged event.

The more that unfolded onscreen, the more Lee-Ann kissed some boy Millie had never even seen, then laughed and thrust out her rapidly developing breasts, the sicker Millie grew.

Acting on autopilot, she reached to Cooper for support, clasping his hand and appreciating his hearty squeeze of hers.

"Mrs. Hansen, I understand you're upset, but I'll need you to sign this document, stating that you've seen the evidence and accept LeeAnn's punishment."

"Of course…" Her hand shook so badly, that she had trouble writing her name.

"I can tell this is a shock to you, but sadly, it's not as uncommon as you might think. Now, I'm not suggesting there's a problem in your home, but I know LeeAnn lost her father at an impressionable age, which can sometimes lead to this sort of reaching out for male attention. The statistics on teen pregnancy are sobering, so you'll want to do everything you can to nip this behavior—"

"Stop right there," Cooper said. "LeeAnn kissed a boy. I think we're a bit premature in declaring her a teenage mom."

While Cooper waged battle on her daughter's behalf, Millie couldn't help but think how ironic it was that she would soon become an unwed mother.

"I'm sorry you feel that way," the principal said in regard to one of Cooper's comments. Millie had been so deep into her own thoughts, she hadn't paid attention to the growing rift between the two men. "Mrs. Hansen, LeeAnn must be present in after-school detention each day next week or face expulsion. You'll be able to pick her up promptly at four thirty-five."

COOPER LED THE two ladies in his life to the truck.

They hadn't even had time to put their seat belts on when Millie lit into her daughter. "What do you think you were doing? You're too young for kissing—let alone, kissing at school."

Her daughter had the gall to roll her eyes. "God, Mom, I'm almost twelve."

"Yeah, well, if you plan on making it to the ripe old age of thirteen, you'd better cut that sass."

Cooper reversed out of their parking spot and headed home.

"You're so lame," LeeAnn fired back. "Uncle Cooper knew I made out with Damon, and he didn't care."

Cooper tightened his grip on the wheel. Did his niece seriously just rat him out?

"What?" Millie swung her attention back to him. "Is that true?"

"Yes and no. It's complicated, and she promised she'd never do it again."

"She *promised?* Lee's eleven! Didn't you ever lie to your parents to get out of trouble? Only, that's right, you're not her parent, are you?"

"No..." Because Millie was understandably upset, he'd give her a pass on scolding him. He was more pissed at himself and his niece.

"Then if you caught my daughter doing something she shouldn't have been, why didn't you tell me?"

"Truth? I wanted her to like me."

Millie covered her face with her hands. "A parent doesn't have that luxury, Cooper."

"Guys, please stop fighting." LeeAnn had started crying, but Cooper suspected they were crocodile tears. "Mom, Uncle Cooper did yell at me when he caught me in the hall kissing Damon."

"When?" Millie inquired.

"The night of the science fair. Damon asked me to be his girlfriend, and said I had to kiss him."

"Cooper," Millie asked, "from the start, tell me what you know that I don't."

He sighed while zigzagging through traffic. "Look, that night, when we separated to find the kids, I stumbled across Lee and this punk. They were kissing, and I told her quite clearly to knock it off. She promised she'd never do it again. End of story."

"See, Mom?" LeeAnn braced her arms over the extended cab's front seat. "He didn't even care."

Millie snapped, "Sit back and put on your seat belt."

"Oh—I cared, all right," Cooper said to LeeAnn. "The only reason I didn't tell your mom was because she's already stressed enough. If you'd held up your end of the bargain, no one ever needed to know."

"Now you're stooping so low as to bargain with an eleven-year-old?"

"It wasn't like that," he said. Only seeing the incident now through Millie's eyes, he saw that it was. If he'd practiced full disclosure back in February, they wouldn't be fighting now. "I told her to stop, and never kiss again."

"Sure." Millie crossed her arms. "That makes about as much sense as if your father had told you to never drink again after you'd run down your mother. How could I be so stupid as to think you're even half the man your brother was? Jim might not have been flashy, but he was good. He knew better than to turn a blind eye to an eleven-year-old making out!"

On that dirty note, Cooper whipped her truck onto the busy highway's shoulder and killed the engine. "Did you honestly just go there? What happened with my mom has nothing to do with this. But you know what, Mill? If due to my lack of expert parental judgment, you're uncomfortable with me being around your kids, I'll be happy to take off first thing in the morning— that is, assuming you're okay with a screwup like me staying the night?"

"SORRY TO BARGE in like this," Millie said to Lynette a little over an hour later. "I didn't know where else to turn."

"Of course." Lynette drew her into the simple ranch house she shared with Zane. "You know you're welcome here anytime."

Millie nodded while making her way to the sofa. Even though she'd delivered her big speech to Cooper, she'd been so upset that the moment he'd parked she'd run off, leaving him to watch Clint and the kids. She was such a hypocrite, accusing him of being a rotten uncle when she wasn't exactly Mother of the Year. "I told you the basics of our fight over the phone, but I kind of left off the reason why Cooper and Lee's secret hit me so hard."

"Okay…" Her friend sat beside her.

"Is Zane in the house?"

"Nope. Can you believe it? He's out for a run. He's

getting pretty buff." Lynette fanned herself. "God bless Cooper and his SEAL Session workout."

Millie rolled her eyes. She was not in the mood for singing Cooper's praises.

"So? What did you need to talk about? We have the house to ourselves and I'm all ears."

Where do I start?

Chapter Seventeen

"C-calm down." Clint sat in the straight-backed chair next to Cooper's dresser. How his father had even gotten up the stairs was beyond him, but stubborn had always been Clint's middle name. "M-Millie didn't mean it. G-girl's got a w-wicked temper. S-stay."

"Love to, Dad, but I can't. I needed to be back on base a month ago." But more important, if he had to spend one more day around Millie, pretending he felt nothing for her but platonic affection, he'd go freakin' mad.

He felt awful about what had gone down with Lee-Ann. Millie was clearly right in that he had no business being around kids. The crazy thing was, though, the more he'd been around his niece and nephew, the more he craved being with them.

He'd miss them when he was gone.

"M-marry her."

"Dad…" Clint scooped the meager contents from his sock drawer into his duffel.

"I m-mean it. Worth a t-try."

"When—if—I ever get married, I don't want to just try, but really make it work. I want what Jim and Millie used to have. The perfect family."

His dad shook his head. "N-no such thing as p-perfect. All m-marriage is w-work."

"I don't know… You and Mom looked pretty good."

Clint smiled. "Your m-mom was a s-saint. I was the p-problem. S-stay. Give M-Millie—yourself—time. She looks at you l-like your m-mom once looked at m-me."

Cooper wished he could believe that, but he knew better.

Millie didn't want him, but to recreate what she'd shared with his brother. Unfortunately, as she'd been all too happy to point out, he'd never be half the man his brother had been.

"WHOA…" LYNETTE FINISHED her wine in one big gulp. "I never saw this one coming. You and Cooper on the kitchen table? That's hot stuff…" She refilled her glass and took another deep swig. "You have to tell him about the baby, Mill. Like, now."

"But how? Especially after he came right out and said he doesn't have any interest in becoming a dad. And what about this thing with LeeAnn? He should've come to me right away about something that important."

"Agreed, but, sweetie, you have to understand that he hasn't been around kids since he was a kid himself. You can't expect him to right out of the gate be *WonderDad*."

"I know, but—"

"No—there's nothing more for you to say. You have to tell him. March your butt straight home and admit you've been scared about how he'd take the news, but that you're sorry, and would like to have an adult conversation about how the two of you plan to raise this child."

Millie nibbled her pinkie fingernail. "You do know you sound like a female *Dr. Phil?*"

"Good. You need some sense drilled into you, and since he's not available for consultation, guess I'll have to do." She stood, taking Millie by her hands to force her from the couch then push her toward the door. "Tell him. *Now.*"

"BUT WHY DO you have to go?" J.J. asked once Cooper had loaded his truck and was ready to hit the highway. "I love you."

"I love you, too, bud." He knelt, wrapping his nephew in a hug.

J.J. tossed his chubby little arms around Cooper's neck and wouldn't let go. "Please, don't leave us. I thought you were going to be our dad."

"Sorry, dude, but you already had a great dad. I'm just your uncle. I promise I'll come visit, but you don't really need me to stay. You've got Grandpa Clint and your mom and sister and friends. Trust me, you'll hardly even notice I'm gone." Still holding J.J., Cooper stood then pushed open the screen door.

"Yes, I will…" The sniffling boy held on tighter.

Clint and LeeAnn followed them outside.

Seemed like just yesterday when Cooper had returned on that blustery January morning. The earth had felt as dead as he had. Everything had been cold and brown and dull. Now, on this night, crickets chirped, the temperature was downright balmy and, just as Millie promised back in March, everything in their world was green and fresh and new. Everything, that is, except for him. He was leaving this ranch feeling as defeated as when he'd come.

LeeAnn asked, "Uncle Cooper, are you leaving because of me?" The girl's question shredded what little remained of his heart.

"Lord, angel, no. I need to get back to the Navy. I know you and your mom will work all of this out. Just please try not to grow up so fast, okay? Promise, you'll have plenty of time for boys once you hit high school. But even then, I'll expect you to shoot me an email about them—you know, just so I can run a background check and make sure they're okay."

As moths danced in the porch lights' glow, she laughed through tears—this time, genuine.

Cooper's eyes stung, and if he hadn't had such a tight hold on his precious nephew, he'd have wiped them. As it was, he just let his tears fall. "I love you guys, so much. Be good for your mom, okay?"

"I will," J.J. said when Cooper set him down.

"C-call when you get there safe." Clint moved in for a hug. "I l-love you, son."

"Love you, too, Dad."

"P-please come home s-soon."

"I will. First chance I get leave." He had to cut this off. He'd seen enough of his SEAL buddies leaving their families to know long goodbyes only dragged out the inevitable. "All right, guys…" He gave all of them one last hug. "I should get going. Talk to you soon."

He walked to his truck on wooden legs. He didn't want to go. The whole time he'd been on the ranch, he'd kept a part of himself back in Virginia. But now? He'd give anything if he and Millie could've worked past their issues and made a go at being a couple. He would've taken it slow. He would do anything for her—

including leaving, because she'd told him that was what she wanted.

The sound of tires crunching on gravel alerted him to there being another vehicle on the drive. He glanced that way to see Millie behind her truck's wheel.

Damn. He'd hoped to have been gone before she got home.

She parked alongside him, her expression startled when she looked in the truck bed to find his duffel, ditty bag and a few boxes of mementos he wanted with him. The beach diorama J.J. had made for him was precious cargo, so it rode on the front seat.

"Are you leaving tonight? Now?" she asked.

J.J. bounded down the front porch stairs. "Mommy, please make him stay! *Please.*"

She hefted her crying son into her arms. "Honey, I wish I could, but Uncle Cooper has a very important job. The whole country needs him—not just us."

If only for a second he thought that was true—that Millie needed him, wanted him—dynamite couldn't have pried Cooper from this place.

"I don't care…" J.J. grew inconsolable.

"LeeAnn, could you please take your brother." Millie set J.J. down, kissing both of his tearstained cheeks, before aiming him toward the house. "Clint, I need a minute alone with Cooper. If you all have said your goodbyes, do you think you could watch the kids for a few minutes while I say mine?"

"W-will do." Clint ushered the kids inside.

"What do you want?" Cooper asked. He was sorry if his sharp words came off as cruel, but she hadn't exactly been a sweetheart to him—more like a lipstick-wearing rattler.

"We need to talk. I thought you weren't leaving till the morning?"

"Plans change."

"Coop…"

"What, Millie? I can't think of another thing you could say to me that hasn't already been said." Unless she wanted to admit she did feel something for him, and that she was as tired of pretending she didn't as he was. Otherwise, he was done.

"Well…" She licked her lips. "I'm not sure where to start."

"Then let's leave it at that."

Her eyes pooled. She opened her mouth, but no words came out, only a strangled sob.

He took it as his sign to go. Didn't she have any idea how crazy he was about her? If she'd given the faintest green light, he'd have retired from the Navy to stay. But she hadn't, and he'd grown weary of trying to please her when clearly, in her eyes, nothing he could ever do would be right.

"Goodbye, Millie." Before his own tears fell, he climbed in the truck. He refused to give her the satisfaction of seeing him fall apart.

But he did—fall apart, cry and punch the damn wheel.

He mourned not only the people he was leaving behind, but also his future that no longer held the slightest appeal. He'd joined the Navy looking for an escape, but all he wanted now was to be found.

Brewer's Falls—Millie, J.J., LeeAnn and his dad—were his home.

Driving through town, he now saw the appeal. Like him, with the changing seasons, it'd been reborn. Cascading flower baskets hung from every light post, and empty shop fronts had been filled with flea-market-style booths of seasonal wares. Potted flowers lined the sidewalks. Mack's bar and the restaurant had set out picnic tables—all currently filled by couples and families dining under the stars.

Cooper wanted so badly to once again be part of this place, but it just wasn't meant to be. And so he sped up, hoping the more miles he put between him and his pain, the better off he'd feel.

AFTER THE GLOW from Cooper's truck's taillights had faded, Millie didn't seek the comfort of her children or father-in-law to cry out her frustration. Instead, she went to the one place where she felt most connected to Cooper—the chicken palace he'd created.

She sat sideways on the swing, barefoot with her knees drawn to her chest.

Why hadn't she told him? She knew Cooper. One hint about her pregnancy would've kept him on the ranch. But what then? Would he marry her? Only to live out the rest of their lives resenting each other for being saddled in a loveless match? She deserved better. She demanded better.

Trouble was, only with the finality of watching him drive away did she realize she did love him—with every breath of her being. He was the first thing she thought of in the morning, and the last thing at night. Of course her kids meant the world to her, but somehow Cooper had also earned his way inside their world, only he didn't seem to know it.

She cupped her hands to her belly, connecting with the tiny life inside. Would she tell Cooper before or after their child's birth? She assumed once she did tell him that he'd want to be part of their baby's future, but what if deep down he didn't? He'd told her parenting sounded like a nightmare. Did she really want a man with that kind of attitude around her newborn?

Eyes closed, she prayed for peace, but her stomach kept churning with the phrase *I should've told him.*

THE NEXT DAY Cooper made it to St. Louis before needing a nap.

He'd always been fascinated by the Arch, so he pulled off I-70 to crash in the grassy park. To say his mood was dark would be an understatement. Judging by the amount of hyper kids and chasing parents, he'd have been better off at a grungy truck stop.

After finding a shady spot under a tree, he tried shutting his eyes, but his mind kept replaying J.J.'s crying plea for him to stay. Or the way LeeAnn had assumed her wrongdoing had been the cause for his leaving when nothing could be further from the truth.

He wanted the responsibility for his hasty departure solely on Millie, but that wouldn't be true.

When they'd made love, everything changed. They'd unleashed a genie that couldn't be put back in its bottle.

Even if he'd wanted to, he couldn't stop wanting her. But no—there was more to it than that. What he felt went deeper, with an infinite number of layers. He could be furious with her one moment, but still crave talking with her the next. He loved everything about her, from her hair to her laugh and smile. The way she smelled all flowery with a hint of sweet. He loved her kids and her house that'd once been his. And damn, did he love her kisses…

What did all of that add up to? Was he losing his mind, or could he possibly be *in love* with her?

That thought forced him upright.

Bracing his hands behind him, he stared out at the Mississippi River, breathing in the rich, musky smell.

I love Millie.

The solution to his every problem was so simple, he felt stupid for not having seen it before. But there it was. His entire adult life, he'd been trained to handle any situation with maximum efficiency and minimum effort, so why couldn't he apply those same ideals to a mule-stubborn woman?

On his feet, he strode to his truck with new purpose.

He had a lot of miles to go, but once he reached his destination, if his plan went the way he hoped, he might not travel again for a nice, long while.

IT'D BEEN AGES since Millie had checked the cattle on horseback, but with Cooper gone, Sassy needed the exercise, and she needed fresh air to help her forget his leaving. It'd barely been twenty-four hours since he'd been gone, but she still couldn't seem to swallow past the knot in her throat.

It didn't help that she'd been up half the night, trying to console J.J. He didn't understand how the man he'd grown to love could leave him. Millie tried explaining about Cooper's job, but he was too young to understand.

LeeAnn hadn't fared much better.

And then there was poor Clint. The only time Millie had seen him cry since losing Jim was after Cooper drove away.

Millie had needed to be strong for her family, but how could she with Cooper's son or daughter growing inside? She should've told him. He deserved to know. But pride had gotten in the way. She couldn't bear begging for his affection.

The day was beautiful, with the temperature near eighty. The sky kissed the snow-capped Rockies, and a light breeze swayed the rolling prairie's tall grasses. She should've been tipping her head back, drinking in the sun. Instead, she focused on reaching the herd. She carefully counted heads then checked that they all looked healthy. This time of year, there was plenty of grass for them to graze on, and they drank from the spring-fed ponds.

With her work done, she sat back in the saddle, taking in the view.

How different would her life be if she had told Cooper about the baby? Would he be here with her now?

From this part of the family land, she had a clear view of their dirt road. A dust cloud rose at the end nearest town. Was the vehicle a neighbor approaching, or maybe the FedEx man—feeding Lynette's catalog addiction?

Millie began the short ride back to the barn, keeping an eye on the vehicle as it approached, glad for the distraction of getting her mind off Cooper and her sense of loss. She hadn't realized how much she'd appreciated his compliments about her cooking or appearance. Then there were those sexy, slow grins. He wasn't just handsome, but kind—not only to her, but her kids.

From her vantage, still a good half mile from the house, it looked as if the vehicle on the road had turned into their drive.

Once the dust settled, a black Ford truck that looked an awful lot like Cooper's sat parked in his usual spot.

Her chest tightened. Was she seeing a mirage?

Though the doctor told her riding should be safe as long as she didn't try anything fancy, Millie quickened Sassy's pace not quite to a gallop, but at least faster than her casual mosey.

Could it really be him?

If so, why? Had he forgotten something?

The ten-minute ride seemed to take forever, but when she finally reached the barn, she was gifted by an incredible sight.

There stood Cooper in all his glory—faded jeans, black T-shirt and his beat-up straw hat, which, to his credit, he removed when she approached.

"Hey," he said, taking Sassy's reins.

Millie gingerly climbed off her ride. "Hey, yourself. Forget something?"

He took a step forward, and then another until before Millie had time to process what was happening, Cooper cupped her cheek and kissed her. "Hell, yeah, I forgot something—you. I love you. And before you go and throw out some excuse why we shouldn't be together, I want to tell you why we should. You're beautiful and you and J.J. and Lee make me so happy. I said I didn't want kids, but I lied. I want dozens—but only if they're yours and mine—*ours.*"

Was this really happening? Millie's eyes welled and the tension that had caused a constant knot in her stomach vanished. "You love me?"

"Yes." He took a step back, adopting a defensive posture. Hands out, as if welcoming a fight, he said, "Come on, I'm sure you have an argument all loaded up to shoot, but I'm not having it. We're going to get married and that's that. I'm not taking no for an answer."

Millie's emotions had gotten the best of her, and all she felt capable of doing was crying.

"Well? What do you have to say?"

So much. But nothing seemed to matter other than kissing him again. Even though she hadn't gone anywhere, pressing her lips against him felt akin to coming home. In only a few short months, he'd come to mean the world to her, but then hadn't he always in one way or another? For as long as she could remember, they'd always been friends. Now, they'd just change their status to friends with benefits and kids.

"That was nice," he said when they paused for air, "but you still haven't answered my question."

She bowed her head. "First, there's something you need to know. For weeks, I've tried finding the right way to say this, but I kept flubbing it up. Anyway…" After forcing a deep breath, she blurted, "I'm pregnant."

For a second he looked pale, but then his color returned along with a broad smile. "For real?"

She nodded. "Is that okay?" Such a stupid question. Even if it wasn't—okay—there wasn't a whole lot they could do about it now.

"Oh, sugar, it's way more than okay…" Dropping Sassy's reins, Cooper hugged her, lifting her feet off the ground to spin her in a slow circle, all the while kissing her till she wasn't sure how she'd ever lived without this man's love. After setting her to her feet, he tossed his hat high and let out a whoop. "I'm gonna be a daddy!"

Hands pressed to her flushed cheeks, Millie wasn't sure whether to laugh, cry or both. "I was so afraid to tell you. The last thing I wanted was for you to feel trapped. You've got your career back in Virginia. What're you going to do?"

"I've put about twelve hours of thought into that and I want to run something past you. That cattle auction I scheduled should bring in a pretty penny, but not enough to get the ranch totally out of the red. Plus, we'll have some lean years while we rebuild the herd. What would you think if I retire from the Navy so we can open a sideline business?"

"What were you thinking? Teaching riding lessons?"

"Bigger." He grinned. "You know how I've been helping Zane and some of our other friends work off their beer bellies?"

She nodded.

"Okay, picture this—we'll build a bunkhouse, and an obstacle course, and then run weekend retreats for guys—and gals—who want to push themselves hard enough to see if they have what it takes to be a SEAL. What do you think?"

"I think most anything you do sounds great to me."

He drew her into another kiss so hot she was surprised the ground didn't have scorch marks beneath her boots. "I love you, Millie Hansen."

"Mmm…" They kissed again. "I love you, Cooper Hansen."

"When we get married," he teased, "are you gonna keep your last name?"

She feigned deep thought. "Being a modern girl, I might go with a hyphen."

"Anyone ever told you you're a sassy little thing?"

The horse heard her name and neighed.

"Uh-oh." Millie laughed. "Looks like I have competition for your affections."

Cooper waved off her concern. "I'm man enough

for both of you. So where are the kids? I want to tell them our news."

She gasped. "Oh, no! I totally forgot. Remember Lee's detention? They're both still at school."

After a quick run inside to tell Clint their news, Millie was all too happy to sit alongside Cooper while he broke a few speed laws to get them to Wagon Wheel Elementary in time.

At school, Cooper took Millie's hand, giving her a light squeeze. "Ready?"

"Absolutely. They're going to be so excited."

Since the detention kids still had five more minutes, they found J.J. in the library.

He caught sight of his uncle and rocketed in his direction, colliding into him. "You came back!"

"I love you and your mom and sister too much to stay away." Cooper lifted the boy into his arms for a hug. "I'm sorry I left you for even one night."

"It's okay." J.J. rested his head on his uncle's shoulder. When he closed his teary eyes, his smile was so serene that Millie had to grab a few tissues from the librarian's desk to blot her own eyes.

The happy trio went to find LeeAnn in the cafeteria.

"Uncle Cooper?" She had the same reaction as her little brother, running to hug him.

"I missed you," Cooper said. "Have any pretty dresses?"

"A few. Why?"

Millie couldn't contain her own excitement. "We'll have to get you a new one. That is, if you'll agree to be my maid of honor."

"Wait—are you two getting married?" LeeAnn

looked to her mom, then her uncle. "But would that make Uncle Cooper our dad?"

"Your stepdad," he said. "Your real dad should come first in your heart, but I hope you'll save a little room for me."

"Well, yeah, but..." She stopped to cross her arms. "Does this mean you're always going to be around to see if I'm with boys?"

"Yes, ma'am."

She groaned. "Mom, is it too late to call the wedding off?"

"Afraid so." Millie slipped her arm around her daughter's shoulders and laced her fingers with Cooper's. The happiness inside her was indescribable. She'd never dreamed of getting a second chance at love, but here it was, all shiny and new and hers for the taking. All she had to do was get her cowboy SEAL to a preacher. And she planned on accomplishing that pretty darned fast. "I've got my heart set on becoming a June bride."

"Cool!" On their walk to the truck, J.J. took Cooper's hat and set it on his own head. "Can we have wedding cake?"

"You bet," Cooper said.

"And punch?"

He kissed her son's freckled cheek. "All you want."

"Wait a minute," Millie interjected. "Don't drink so much that you get sick. I'm not sure about having to take a sick little boy along on our honeymoon."

"How about if J.J. promises to drink just enough punch that he doesn't get sick, then we all go on a *familymoon?*"

LeeAnn wrinkled her nose. "What's that?"

Cooper opened the back door of the truck. "A *family-*

moon will be our very own invention. To celebrate our wedding, I think we should all go somewhere fun."

"The zoo?" J.J. suggested.

"Mount Vesuvius?" LeeAnn tossed out.

"How about Disney World?" Cooper said.

By unanimous decision, the Magic Kingdom was deemed the perfect spot to begin their magical new lives.

Epilogue

To celebrate her and Cooper's first wedding anniversary, Millie had wanted to throw an elegant dinner party in the front yard. She'd dreamed of stringing romantic white lights in the trees and having hundreds of flickering candles.

What she got was a seat on a hard rodeo arena stand, sitting alongside a very pregnant Lynette.

J.J. and LeeAnn were off playing with friends, and Millie jiggled Cooper Junior on her knee. He was already a handful, but just like his father, he was so cute, she didn't much mind.

Cooper's business venture had gone better than even he'd imagined, and his SEAL strength-building and self-protection retreats were already booked into the next year.

"Think they'll win?" Lynette asked when Cooper and Zane were in their respective chutes.

"I don't know," Millie said, "but they sure look good in those red shirts."

While professional team calf ropers got the job done in as little as 3.5 seconds, it took their guys 6.7.

"Sorry we couldn't pull out the win for you." Cooper took his son, sweeping him high in the air.

Millie was next in line for his attention with a leisurely kiss. As handsome as he was, Cooper was a fan favorite on their local rodeo circuit, but Millie was proud to be the only recipient of his kisses.

Clint strode up to shake both men's hands. He'd made a full recovery and had as much fun at rodeos as his son. "Fine ride, boys. You made me proud. You'll pull out a win next time."

"Thanks, Dad." Cooper shifted the baby to his other arm. "Would you mind watching this guy for a minute?"

"Is it time?" Clint asked with an exaggerated wink.

"Time for what?" Millie asked.

"Thanks for keeping a secret, Dad."

Clint grinned while jiggling his grandson. "We didn't tell your momma a thing, did we?"

Cooper drew Millie off into the shadows. "Damn, you look hot."

"Thanks, cowboy." She gave him a kiss. "You're looking mighty fine yourself."

"I appreciate that, ma'am, but tonight, being our first anniversary, I wanted you to know how much I love you, and how this has pretty much been the best year of my life."

"Aw…" Her husband's sweet talk never failed to make her heart sing. "Thank you, honey. I love you, too."

"Okay, so you know how we pretty much had a budget wedding?"

"I thought our day was beautiful. Marrying you under your mom's rose trellis was the only place I'd have wanted it to be."

"I'm glad," he said, acting all fidgety, "but now that we've finally got a little extra money, I want you to have this. It's high time you had something to really show you're mine."

From his shirt pocket, he withdrew a small, mangled paper sack, and handed it to her.

Hoping she was doing a good job of masking her confusion, she smiled. "Thanks?"

"Go ahead. Open it." He grinned like a kid on Christmas morning.

She unrolled the paper to find a lopsided Oreo. "You got me a cookie?"

His smile only grew. "Eat it."

"Okay?" She started to bite into it, then he drew her hand down. "Not like that. You've got to twist it apart, then lick the icing—only, be careful. I don't want you to get hurt."

"Honey, you're acting strange. Are you sure you didn't get hurt during your run?"

Sighing, he said, "Would you go ahead and lick the damn cookie?"

She laughed. "Sorry. You don't have to get all huffy."

"Then lick, and I won't have to."

Finally doing his bidding, she twisted the top off her favorite treat then gasped. It wouldn't even take one lick to see Cooper had hidden a diamond ring in the icing.

Squealing, she kissed him, licked the ring, gobbled part of the cookie, then kissed him again. "Put it on for me?"

He did. In the process, kissing her hand, then lips.

"This is beyond gorgeous," she said, gazing at the square-cut diamond. "You shouldn't have."

"Want me to take it back?" he teased.

"Just try, and see what happens."

"There you go again with that sass." He drew her tight against him, bowing his head to kiss her good and thorough beneath his wide hat brim.

"Eeew!" J.J. came tearing around the corner with his friend Cayden in tow. "You guys are gross!"

LeeAnn and Kara followed.

LeeAnn asked, "Did you give Mom her ring and the trip?"

He conked his head. "I forgot the trip."

Both kids laughed.

J.J. started jumping. "Show her! Show her!"

From his back pocket, he produced with a flourish a slip of paper. "Since our honeymoon got hijacked, and you're always talking about how much you'd like to see the world, how about a second honeymoon to Machu Picchu?"

"You mean the ruins? In Peru?"

Grinning, he said, "Those would be the ones."

That earned him another kiss!

Millie asked, "Did everyone know I was getting all of this, but me?"

"Pretty much." Her daughter and friend laughed while admiring her bauble.

"Thank you," she said to her husband once the kids had run off again. "Not just for the ring and trip, but for coming home—for staying home."

"Mill…" He cupped her face with his hands. "Haven't you figured it out? You and the kids are my home. You're my everything."

Millie rested her head on her husband's shoulder while they sauntered hand in hand back into the crowd. What a great night. What a great life. Spying a shooting star, she thanked Jim for sending her his brother—her very own cowboy SEAL.

* * * * *

MILLS & BOON®

Power, passion and irresistible temptatio

The Modern™ series lets you step into a worl
of sophistication and glamour, where sinfully
seductive heroes await you in luxurious
international locations. Visit the Mills & Boor
website today and type **Mod15** in at
the checkout to receive

15% OFF

your next Modern purchase.

Visit **www.millsandboon.co.uk/mod15**